D0773212

BEHIND EVERYMAN

BEHIND EVERYMAN

a novel

for guys

and the

women who

rescue them

DAVID ISRAEL

BALLANTINE BOOKS · NEW YORK

CARLSBAD CITY LIBRARY

DISCARD

ISRAEL, D.

Behind Everyman is a work of fiction. Names, characters, places, and incidents are the products of the author's imagination or are used fictitiously. Any resemblance to actual events, locales, or persons, living or dead, is entirely coincidental.

A Ballantine Books Trade Paperback Original

Copyright © 2005 by David Israel

All rights reserved.

Published in the United States by Ballantine Books, an imprint of The Random House Publishing Group, a division of Random House, Inc., New York.

Ballantine and colophon are registered trademarks of Random House, Inc.

Grateful acknowledgment is made to ABKCO Music, Inc. for permission to reprint an excerpt from "Sympathy For the Devil," written by Mick Jagger and Keith Richards. Published by ABKCO Music, Inc. (BMI).

Library of Congress Cataloging-in-Publication Data
Israel, David, 1967–
Behind everyman : a novel for guys and the women who rescue them / by David Israel.—1st trade pbk. ed.
p. cm.
1. Young men—Fiction. 2. Screenwriters—Fiction. 3. New York (N.Y.)—Fiction. 4. Underemployment—Fiction. I. Title.
PS3609.S59B44 2005
813'.6—dc22   2004053841

ISBN 0-345-47660-3

Printed in the United States of America

www.ballantinebooks.com

1 2 3 4 5 6 7 8 9

First Edition: February 2005

Text design by Susan Turner

MAY 2 3 2005

CARLSBAD CITY LIBRARY
DISCARD

FOR MY PARENTS, LINDA AND MILT

CONTENTS

WHY DON'T WRITERS ever name their protagonists Bob? Why must they always be Holdens, Seths, Earnests, or Jays? Even when they could be named Bob, they wind up being called Robert, or Rob. Why is that? This is a question that has puzzled the author for some time.

Maybe the answer, like the answers to most questions, can be found in the Bible—the number one selling book of all time. Maybe in an attempt to generate sales of equal magnitude, writers feel that unique or obscure one-of-a-kind names will give their novels an edge. Admittedly, Ezechiel, Ashhur, and Zipporah are pretty slick names. And, sure, it's hard to imagine the Book of Job beginning:

> *There was a man in the land of Uz, whose name was Bob; and that man was blameless and upright, one who*

feared God, and turned away from evil. There were born to him seven sons and three daughters.

He had seven thousand sheep, three thousand camels, five hundred yoke of oxen, and five hundred she-asses, and very many servants; so that Bob was the greatest of all the people of the east.

As for this book, the problem of naming the protagonist has been eliminated. He is you or your cousin Phil. He is your old college pal Owen or the quiet guy who lives in the apartment above you—the one who gets all those magazine subscriptions in unmarked brown paper envelopes.

The protagonist is Everyman, and as such, he has no name. Feel free to give him one if you'd like. Feel free to give him physical characteristics as well and dress him as you please. (Sort of like you did with your old G.I. Joe. Remember? When, just for fun, you put your sister's Barbie dress on him? Yeah. Like that. Go ahead, admit it. You did too. It's okay. We all did.)

Neither the author nor his publisher guarantee that the advice contained in this novel will make you as savvy and debonair as Everyman. On the other hand, it very well might. It all depends on how open you are to change and, of course, to what degree you already consider yourself a raging failure.

It bears noting that this is a work of fiction. Any resemblance to real people or occurrences is strictly coincidental—except, of course, the bit about the protagonist's mother biting her toenails. The author couldn't have come up with something more hilarious if he tried. Apologies in advance, then, to Mom—but a heartfelt and sincere thanks nonetheless, as the Beastie Boys once said, "for bringing me into this world, and so on."

—*David Israel*

BEHIND EVERYMAN

HOW TO BEGIN A SCREENPLAY

I

START BY GETTING a liberal arts degree from a college like Penn State—or any such similar school where the emphasis of study is firmly placed on fraternal life and sporting events. Because you'll have spent your eight semesters tottering through various degrees of inebriation, upon graduation you'll have little to no idea what to do with your degree. After a few minutes of contemplation, decide to do what everyone else does—move to New York City and take a job in advertising, marketing, or PR.

Your first few months in the city will be overwhelming. Adjusting to life in an apartment so tiny you can touch all four walls simultaneously won't be easy. Throw in a bipolar German roommate named Ulf, who requests the place to himself each and every Wednesday and Sunday evening so he can *geshlugen* with his girlfriend, Nanette, and you'll begin to wonder if you should have thought twice about moving to Manhattan.

Meanwhile, at work, you'll begin to grow tired of expressions like: "At the end of the day" and "You're not thinking outside the box here." You'll begin to question a future where everything must always be, as Ulf once remarked, "Crisp-and-crunch-and-April-fresh!"

After a couple years, colleagues will receive promotions you thought were yours. The assistant vice president position you were coveting will go to Wayne Christodoulou—a man who, after three years, still hasn't taken the 100% Real Wool tag off the cuff of his winter coat.

Within six years, start to regret wasting $100,000+ of your parents hard-earned money on eight semesters of courses like "Comparative Video Gaming." Remember how your father, a successful lawyer, had high hopes for you. Recall with a modicum of bittersweet nostalgia how he once referred to you as "a chip off the old block." Feel like a dismal failure. Fall into a state of minor depression. Wonder if you'll be the next person to rely on Prozac just to get through the day.

When your boss calls you in for your midyear review and tells you that "you're just not applying yourself enough" on the new copy for the Depend diaper campaign, feel like you've hit rock bottom. Wonder how it's come to pass that at the tender age of twenty-eight you've already fallen into the Where-Are-They-Now category and have no girlfriend to boot.

———•———

Fret not, for around this time, a brochure will arrive in the mail from The New School announcing adult continuing education courses. At home, sitting on the toilet, begin to thumb through the contents. Circle classes that catch your eye, that pique your curiosity, that cost less than $1,000 per semester and seem like something hot chicks might also enroll in.

The next day at work, use your lunch hour to get the lowdown on a certain screenwriting course that starts in a few weeks. You like going to the movies and you once took a creative writing course in college, so you figure why not combine the two and make a few million while you're at it.

Call up the admissions department and be placed on hold. Settle into your Posturepedic high back with adjustable lumbar support and toy with a paper clip, stretching it out so that it resembles a pubic hair. Hum along with the hold music—any one of 72,000 maudlin ballads by Phil Collins. Tap your pencil.

When the woman from the admissions department comes back on, learn that there's only one opening left. Waste no time by giving her your credit card and social security number. Then ask: "So what's the ratio of boys to girls again?"

Next, call up your parents and tell them the good news. They'll say, "That's my boy!" and "Well, whaddaya know?!" They'll also ask how June is, the girl you had the one-hour stand with several weeks ago.

Say: "First of all, her name was May, and second of all, I told you it's been over for quite a while."

Listen to a depressing round of "oh, well, that's too bad's" and deflated "well, whaddaya know's" as the mood becomes somber.

Your boss, a woman named Raychel (yes, spelled with a y) with a heavy Staten Island Judaic accent, will stick her head into your office at this time and announce in a deafening voice that she needs to see you, "AYSAYP!"

Begin to count the days until you're a famous screenwriter.

II

THOUGH THERE'S ONLY one girl enrolled in the screenwriting course—a sloppy brunette named Fern, whose face resembles a manhole cover more than it does a vascular houseplant—begin to enjoy the class and note how each week you find yourself looking forward to Tuesdays and Thursdays at 8:15 p.m. with increasing zeal. Find that you take to the discipline of turning in your required three pages of script a day like a duck to water. Learn that hackneyed expressions like "a duck to water" are not allowed in your daily three pages. Learn what *hackneyed* means. Learn all about "the climax," "the turning point," and "the twist."

Discover that all films are created in three acts and that most follow predictable formulas that someone named Syd out in Hollywood discovered some forty-seven years ago. These formulas have been netting producers and studios so much money for such a long period of time that no one, not even Syd, recommends deviating from them.

Find yourself watching movies like *The Shawshank Redemption, Chinatown,* and *Citizen Kane*—looking to see what happens at the end of the first act.

"Something huge and life altering *must* occur at the end of the first act," your teacher will say, "and it *must* happen twenty minutes into the film or else you'll lose your audience."

Every time he stresses the word *must,* he'll slam his fist down on the desk like Joseph Stalin might have were he teaching a screenwriting course at The New School rather than signing the Nonaggression Pact with his smartly mustached partner. Learn secrets of the trade and special lingo like *sotto voce*—Italian for "in a whisper."

Learn that a script *must* be 120 pages long and that each page generally equals about one minute of actual film time. A rail-thin redheaded fellow in the back of the classroom with a T-shirt that reads "Nuke a Gay Whale for Christ's Sake" will ask what happens if he gets carried away and winds up writing a 200-page script.

Your teacher will bark back: "It *must* be one hundred twenty pages!"

"Yeah, but what if it's two hundred pages?" the gay whale will stubbornly ask again.

"Well," your teacher will say, softening just a bit, "someone in Poland will produce it with subtitles and you might get a cult following out of the thing. But in this class, all scripts *must* be one hundred twenty pages! Is that clear?!"

Learn that interior and exterior location markings are to be abbreviated INT. and EXT. Learn how to three-hole-punch and bind your scripts with two-inch brass fasteners. Learn which books adapt well into screenplays (*Kramer vs. Kramer,* directed by Robert Benton) and which don't (*Caring for Your Adopted Child,* directed by Woody Allen).

———•———

By the end of the course, realize that your ten-hour-a-day workload over at the advertising agency is not allowing you enough time to develop into the budding screenwriter Joseph Stalin thinks you could be. It would be one thing if you actually enjoyed what you were doing, but as it is, you find the job about as stimulating as producing a urine sample.

It will come quite easily, then, for you to suddenly quit your job, prematurely cash in a ten-year CD your parents had set aside for you, and fly off to Belize for some much needed R&R.

———•———

While in Belize, lazing around idyllically under gentle azure skies, begin to formulate ideas for your first hit screenplay. It will be about a finned monster, you'll determine, that periodically emerges from the sea, flipping and flopping his way into resort towns in Central America, creating general unrest and horror. But, and here's the twist, the monster won't be interested in mindless killing, blood and gore, or any of the usual things monsters are generally preoccupied with. Rather (oh! this is going to make you so famous) it'll be more concerned with making the cover of *National Geographic Magazine*. If a few power lines are downed in the process, so be it, but no one will lose his life in this, the first ever, G-rated horror film. It's perfect!

Get to work planning your Lifetime Achievement Oscar acceptance speech at once. Thank your parents, your best friend, your agent, but not God. Well, perhaps God, but use the word *Ha-shem* instead. People will think you're cool, like when Madonna went and got all Kabbalah on everyone.

———•———

After spending your life savings down in Belize, fly back to NYC and begin job hunting for something that will leave you time to focus on your screenplay and just enough income to cover your rent. Though you'll be wildly overqualified, interview for a simple administrative assistant position in the multimedia department of a large financial firm. You'll have issues with your potential boss because he's at least a year younger than you and shakes your hand so stalwartly that most, if not all, of his cologne transfers from his palm to yours. You'll have further issues with the fact that he has absolutely no facial hair. None whatsoever. Like a woman's, his face will look.

When he asks how your Microsoft Excel and Access skills are, tell him that you've used both quite often in the past and that you're sure, with a little refresher course, it will all come back to you in no time. Of course nothing could be further from the truth. In all actuality, you have no idea how to open these programs, much less any comprehension of what they do. Nevertheless, a job is a job, and, more important, it's *just* a job, not a career move, so any finagling of the truth to obtain said job is therefore not only warranted, but encouraged. Keep this in mind as you humbly accept his offer and spend the rest of the afternoon dousing your hand in lemon juice to get rid of the cologne.

———•———

Over the next few months acclimate to your new admin. asst. position while working on your screenplay at home in the evenings. Find that if you get into the office at 8 a.m., you can leave by 4 p.m., giving you plenty of time to crank out at least three pages a day, perhaps more, depending on the Ulf-Nanette situation.

Struggle with the end of the first act. Know that something major has to happen by the twentieth page or else the script will never see the light of day. Consider having the *National Geographic* reporter fall in love with the monster (whom you've recently named Raychel). Write the act thusly only to realize that you've now shot your wad way too early. Realize that Raychel can't fall in love until the middle of the second act—or what's referred to in the industry as "the sixty-page stretch." The second act is where the characters *must* grow, change, and overcome obstacles—but let's not get ahead of ourselves. You're still on the first act.

III

ONE RAINY EVENING, on your way home from the gym, spot an attractive umbrellaless woman standing on the corner of Tenth and University. You've often fantasized about this moment—wondering if you'd have the guts to follow through when the opportunity presented itself.

Just as you've rehearsed over the years, get up the nerve to say, "Which way are you headed?"

When she replies, "Union Square," tell her that you're headed that way too—a complete fabrication, but it's only a few blocks out of your way and the *Village Voice* she's using to shield the rain is disintegrating quickly.

Her name will be Justine, or perhaps Sheila. No, definitely Justine. She'll be a lawyer on her way home from work.

"I do M and A work," she'll say—as if that's supposed to mean something to you.

She'll be grateful that you shared your umbrella with her and spend far more time saying good-bye at Union Square than one normally would. Take this as a hint and ask if she'd like to meet for coffee or tea sometime.

"I'll meet you for a drink," she'll say, "but let's make it a scotch."

Smile at the thought of this. Only one other person you know drinks scotch. Wonder if kissing her good night on the cheek will remind you of kissing your geriatric grandfather, Mortimer.

———•———

The following week, a beer in your hand, a scotch in hers, discover that Justine left her last boyfriend because she didn't like the way he proposed to her. Or, to clarify, her girlfriends didn't like the way he proposed to her.

"It's not about the size of the stone," she'll say, rattling the ice at the bottom of her glass. "Anyone can throw a lot of money into a ring. It's about the gesture."

Let her chiseled features and ravishing lips blind you from seeing this as a potential problem. Tell her you couldn't agree more—that if you ever proposed to her, you'd jump out of an airplane and parachute onto her roof with a Cracker Jack ring in your teeth.

———•———

Two drinks later, after you've heard all about her three-week vacation in Paris where she spent more time in Chanel than anywhere else, she'll ask what "rocks your world," what "gets you juiced"?

Say: "Oh God. You know. Lots," and take a big swig from your bottle of Guinness.

"Like what?"

Another swig. "Well, let's see. I like sporty things."

"Oh, you mean like Ralph Lauren's Polo line?"

Smile. Wonder what you're doing with this girl.

Say: "Well, no, not exactly. Though I do have a Polo shirt." Of course you do—a lousy knockoff so obvious, even you can tell the difference. The polo guy is supposed to be mounted on a horse, not an aardvark.

She'll down some more scotch and then look at her watch. Force a smile. Feel like an imitation of yourself. Like that radio at your parents' house with the "Genuine Simulated Wood Grain Cabinet" sticker that no one removed.

Tell her that by sporty you mean waterskiing, hiking, basketball, and camping.

"Oh really?" she'll say. "I play racquetball."

Smack your beer down on the table with renewed enthusiasm and say, "No kidding!"

———•———

The following week, discover that "I play racquetball" means "Someone gave me an expensive racquet for my birthday." Flossing your teeth would burn more calories than an hour on the court with Justine. Nevertheless, pretend you're enjoying yourself and, most important, be patient with her. Use the calmest voice at your disposal when explaining for the tenth time the concept of holding on to the racquet after it hits the ball. Remember: It's not about exercise; it's about doing something fun together.

———•———

Later that evening, go to a "fine" sushi place she knows a few blocks from the gym. Discover that "fine" actually means one spicy tuna hand roll costs more than you make in a week.

When she asks why you're not ordering more, say, "Oh, you know. It's hard for me to eat a big meal after such an invigorating workout."

———•———

After you've eaten your lone hand roll and have downed the entire carafe of sake for two, sit quietly as Justine eats.

"So," she'll say in between bites of what looks like the most delicious *unagi* you'll ever pay for, "tell me more about you. What else do you like besides sports?"

Take your time with this one—after all that sake on an empty stomach, thoughts will appear to be much larger than they actually are.

Say: "Children."

"Chinren?" she'll gasp, swallowing a piece of ginger.

You've heard this before. Women always think you're joking around—throwing them the sensitive line just to get them in bed. But you're not. You have a soft spot for children. And according to the women you date, it's unusual.

Nod your head as you repeat, "Mm-hmm. Children."

"Well, that's refreshing to hear," she'll say, suddenly all aglow.

———•———

When the check comes, remarkably, she'll offer to pay half. Think: *You want to talk about what's refreshing to hear? Hot damn!*

"You barely ate anything," she'll say. "It's only fair."

———•———

The following evening, call her to make plans for another date. Be caught off guard when she sounds uninterested.

After some small talk about racquetball accessories, inquire if something's wrong.

"Actually, now that you ask, yes, I'm a bit upset."

"What happened? I thought we had a pretty good time last night."

Stand there stupefied as she explains that she doesn't want to see you anymore. She talked it over with her girlfriends and they convinced her that you're a cheapskate. Not paying for dinner the first time you were out together is a red flag she just can't ignore. She's dated frugal men in the past and she wants no part of it.

"But you offered to pay half. You said I didn't eat much—that it was only fair."

"Yeah, well, I didn't expect you to take me up on it."

According to Justine, she'd rather you take her out to McDonald's and pay the entire bill yourself than take her to a fancy restaurant and expect her to pay half.

"Remember when I told you about my ex?" she'll continue. "Were you listening? It's not about the money; it's about the gesture."

When she drops the obligatory, "Well, have a nice life," hang up wishing she could see the gesture you're presently giving the phone.

IV

AFTER YOU'VE BEEN WORKING at your new job for six months, come to the conclusion that it's truly dull, mindless work, better

suited for those who spend their time in the company of dairy animals. Begin to work on your screenplay in the cracks to liven up
the day. Rig a complex system of mirrors around your cubicle that
allows you to see in every direction—just to make sure your boss
doesn't catch you screwing around.

One day, while on the phone with Ulf, trying to persuade him
to let you use the apartment one night for your annual Stanley
Cup party, notice your boss approaching. Abruptly end the Stanley Cup conversation before the conflict is resolved (read: before
you once again cave to the big-boned schizo). Regard your boss
in the mirrors as you hurriedly click over from Word to Excel.
He'll enter your cubicle and hover over your desk for a few minutes, asking redundant questions about the spreadsheet that's open
on your screen—stealing glances every now and again at your task
bar just to see what files you've got lurking in the background.
Since you've foxily named your screenplay "Vendor Accruals
Fiscal_03.doc," you needn't worry that he'll know what you're
really up to.

V

YOU MAY DISLIKE your boss and you may find the work remarkably uninspiring, but the insurance coverage? Fantastic!

Back at the ad agency, your company plan covered little beyond Band-Aids and a do-it-yourself colonic kit. But now you
have full medical and dental—including full mental health and vi-
sion care with nothing required of you, hold a small out-of-pocket
co-pay. Now you can get those new lenses you've needed. Now
you can get that chipped tooth fixed and lots of free toothbrushes
and floss from the dentist. Begin to feel like you're living in Nor-
way or Sweden, or some other such IKEA-esque place famous for
their health coverage.

Decide that you're sufficiently screwed up to take the plunge into talk therapy. What with your ongoing female problems (lately your relationships have been expiring before the milk in your fridge) and your newfound career as a struggling screenwriter, you deserve to take full advantage of the firm's generous mental health plan.

Begin to make lists of things you need to address in therapy—things that your therapist will later refer to as "baggage that won't fit in the overhead compartment." One day, for instance, you'll be staring out your thirtieth-floor office window, down at the convergence of 65,000 taxicabs into the Times Square area, when suddenly you'll notice a gigantic billboard advertising your latest hit film. But then, in another moment, you'll realize that it's only an ad for the latest Schwarzenegger extravaganza. Put that on your list as you find yourself, once again, feeling like an abject loser who's now approaching twenty-nine, careerless, and working a job that your cousin's son Billy, age eight and a half, could do three years ago.

VI

BEGIN DATING A GIRL named Kaya, who you'll meet in the world music stacks at Tower Records. On the second date, over veggie burgers that taste like asphalt, ask what the name Kaya means. Her eyebrows will nearly jump off her forehead as she screams, "You mean you never heard the Bob Marley song, 'Got to Have Kaya Now'?!"

Lower your head in shame. Fiddle with your French fries. She'll spend the next few minutes telling you all about kaya, or marijuana, and how her parents were big-time flower children in the sixties. The following week, when she doesn't return any of your phone calls, don't take it too hard—you didn't care much for the smell of patchouli anyway.

VII

BY THE TIME autumn rolls around, have a revised first draft of your script completed. Register for the second part of the Joseph Stalin course and stock up on two-inch brass fasteners.

Meanwhile, at the financial firm, get up the guts to ask your boss for an increase in salary. Of all your boss's many talents, creating loose ends for you to tidy up is his greatest. Point this out as you begin your heartfelt plea for that big raise. Notice that your boss always responds in clichés. Ever since you learned in Joseph Stalin's class what *hackneyed* means, you've been hyperaware of them. For instance, when you point out the fact that you were the only new hire who didn't receive a bonus, and that you stayed late on more than one occasion and didn't earn overtime, and that you haven't bought a new pair of pants in well over a year, he'll eye your trousers up and down—all the while pulling at the space where his beard might be were he to ever go through puberty—and say, "Well, I suppose you earned your wings. Just make sure you push the envelope a little more—okay? Keep your nose to the grindstone—okay?"

Celebrate by kicking Ulf out on his big-boned German ass and take the entire seventy-five-square-foot apartment for yourself. Put a lamp where his bed used to be and wonder how on earth the two of you ever split such a teeny little nothing of a living space.

VIII

SHARE YOUR SCRIPT with the class. They'll make self-conscious, portentous comments like, "I don't feel that this character is evolving naturally—he seems a bit contrived to me." Or "The device you're employing in the third-act resolution is sort of trite, isn't it? Did you consider blah-bidy-blah, instead?" Or, as the oldest student in the class (seventy-three years old) puts it, "I wouldn't see this malarkey if you paid me."

Try not to get discouraged or defend Raychel's motivations too much. Jot their criticism down on a pad of paper that you'll later throw out. Feel like a rebel—like a misunderstood artist. Feel dejected, uninterested, cast out. Write, "Fuck this shit" on the sole of your sneaker like you used to in high school.

Speak to Stalin after class. He'll say, "What? Did you expect to get it right the first time?"

Tell him that, indeed, you did. That you'd worked on the thing all summer, revising, rewriting, making sure the structure matched Syd's to a tee. Hold the script open to page twenty, the brilliant end of the first act where Raychel assumes the disguise of a gay whale and flops into town with pierced nipples. Question how anyone could see such a brilliant, well-thought-out twist coming—asking several times if he, indeed, saw the twist coming. Gesture flamboyantly at the two-inch brass fasteners and point out how well the overall packaging of the script looks.

When you've finished your ranting, he'll regard you with a look of annoyed tolerance—the way you tolerate old-timers who feed the pigeons. Then he'll shrug his shoulders with a *hmph* and fish out a business card from his well-worn wallet.

"Here," he'll say nonchalantly, "this is my card. Why don't you send me a fresh copy of your script and I'll pass it along to my agent for a professional's opinion. After all, what do I know?"

He'll put his wallet back into his breast pocket, turn, and walk out of the classroom—glumly running his fingers through his hair.

Feel sorry for Joseph Stalin. Pity him in a "those who can, do" sort of way. Stand alone in the classroom and stare solemnly down at the business card in your hand. Have a two- or three-second interlude wherein you're accepting your Lifetime Achievement award. Make a mental note to discuss what you've recently started calling your "castle-in-the-sky modus operandi" with your therapist as you look at your script lying there on the desk, the high-power fluorescent light forever bouncing off the two-inch brass fasteners.

HOW TO RIDE AN ELEVATOR

I

LEARNING TO RIDE an elevator is like learning to ride a bicycle: Once you learn, you never forget. And just like bicycles, elevators come in a variety of styles, makes, and models, with a bevy of bells and whistles.

For instance, some elevators have folding accordionlike gates that must be shut before the elevator is considered operable. These are generally found in Ireland, the United Kingdom, Russia, and other such countries where people consume alcohol with reckless abandon.

Other elevators have special "door close" buttons that need to be pressed (sometimes repeatedly, especially when you're running late) before the car will move.

Some—like the elevator in the ritzy Central Park West co-op your friend Henry lives in—have shortish, always smiling operating men seated on stools who must be acknowledged with a "Howdy," or a "Whaddaya say?" before the elevator will run. These men are invariably of some undeterminable Hispanic background.

When you step into their car on a boiling hot summer day, eating a banana and say, "So, how do you like the heat?"

They'll say, "No, me no hungry, *gracias.*"

The elevator in your parents' building seems to have a mind of its own—or perhaps a personal vendetta dating back to the time when you passed unspeakably foul-smelling gas within its confines. Whatever the reason, it seems that no matter how many times you lean on the "door close" button or punch your floor button, the thing will most definitely *not* budge until it has decided everyone is in. No matter if it's three o'clock in the morning and you're the only moron awake in the entire building, the elevator will sit there for twelve years just to make sure you aren't accidentally standing in the way of the closing doors. Just to make sure ninety-eight-year-old Dolly Hornflogger from 17J isn't puttering through the vestibule with her walker. Even muttering, "For Christ's sake already!" under your breath won't help.

Once the doors do close, however, the elevator will move with fairly decent speed, getting you up to your floor quickly and in relative comfort. You only wish you could say the same about the elevator in the building where your therapist keeps her office. Probably built in the fifth century B.C., this elevator is most definitely run by a series of antiquated pulleys—no doubt operated by thick-necked men in the basement named Ox or Bull who spend their leisure time head-butting the wall. You could complete eighteen holes of golf with nothing but a putter before this elevator moves five floors.

The elevators at the financial firm where you work are a different breed altogether. They are sleek and streamlined—like elevators in *Star Trek.* The doors open and close with a wispy futuristic *whoosh* and ping softly when they arrive at any given floor. Like those found in many skyscrapers, these elevators are numerous and split into banks that serve different floors. Because you work near the top floor, you'll need to use the last bank of elevators.

If you arrive before the morning rush, say, before 8:30 a.m., you stand a good chance of being the only person in the elevator. Step in and grab on to the handrail as these babies tend to break the sound barrier—catapulting from the lobby to the thirtieth floor in less time than it takes you to belch. When the doors open, take a few seconds to gather your belongings and straighten your tie, for items will have most definitely shifted midflight.

Most mornings, however, you'll fiddle with the snooze button on your alarm clock a few times and won't arrive at work until about 8:32 a.m.—two minutes after what your boss refers to as "PARTY TIME!"

At this hour most if not all of the firm's five thousand employees will be arriving as well. Finding more than a nose length of free space in a car is rare. As you're crammed into the car like Cubans on a refugee boat, the old adage "Cleanliness is next to Godliness" becomes sacred.

Should you find yourself smashed up against the back of a slightly, shall we say, ripe passenger, refrain from screwing up your face in discomfort and instead breathe through your mouth. Though you'll sound like a small Jewish boy with an unfortunate bronchial situation, this will prevent you from fainting into the surrounding pack.

Should you find yourself smushed into the front of some shapely blonde's boobs, do your best to focus on something decidedly less arousing, like Dolly Hornflogger's boobs. In such close quarters, the person a mere eyelash length in front of you need not get an early morning "excuse me" up the backside.

If you find yourself stuck next to a young Wharton grad yapping away with excessive bravado about an upcoming IPO on his cell phone, be sure to switch your weight from one leg to the other in an obvious display of annoyance. Also be sure to get the skinny on the IPO and, if it sounds promising, make a mental note to use the $157 dollars you have in savings to purchase large quantities even though you haven't the faintest idea what an IPO is. If it doesn't sound promising, be sure to tell your boss to purchase large quantities.

If you're the last person in the lobby to enter the car, you'll have to do a 180-degree turn before entering and then step in backward. Note that you'll now be within coke-snorting distance of the cool stainless steel door. When the elevator stops, be sure to get out on each floor, allowing those behind you to exit.

Notice how the car seems to be filling up rather than emptying out each time you do this. This is because of a certain physical law of science, which states that bodies tend to expand when in their normal state of obesity. In laymen's terms: Not wanting to be late for work and faced with no other option, the overweight (read: most everyone in the elevator) will suck it up when forced to and let it all hang out when they're not.

A particularly globular woman who works in Corporate Audit on the thirty-first floor—her sizable horselike mouth working arduously on a piece of gum—will begin to take up most of the room herself as people exit the car. Watch in horror as she expands, puffing out like a blowfish with each group exodus. By the time the car reaches the thirtieth floor, you'll be the only two people left in the elevator. Yet, remarkably, you'll still be squashed up against the back of the cool stainless steel door. As you exit the car, notice the engraved panel toward the bottom of the door, which reads: "Capacity: 3,500 lbs." Raise your eyebrows in amusement as the doors close behind you. Wonder how many more pieces of gum you'd have to put into Corp Audit's mouth before she sent the car crashing to the ground.

Around noontime, take the elevator down to the ninth-floor cafeteria. Notice that the conversation on the way to lunch is dramatically different from what it was at 8:30 in the morning. Early in the morning, eye contact is to be avoided at all costs and dialogue mustn't move beyond talk about the weather.

At lunchtime, though eye contact is still discouraged, it's okay to chitchat thusly while discreetly readjusting your testicles with hand in pocket: "Did you see the memo on the SRT deal? What are they? Masochists?" or the tried-and-true, "Yes, well, I think we've got our ducks in a row now."

It will be hard to keep your voice down, as you'll need to be heard over a chorus of vibrating BlackBerrys, but do try to keep the conversation to a whisper.

Once you have your lunch in hand, head back to the elevator and stand next to a big bear of a man who can't wait to reach his desk before digging in. The whole car will reek of onion rings. Shoot him a quick glance. This will cause him to close the Styrofoam lid, lick his fingers, wipe his hand on his trousers, and pretend like nothing happened. Stare blankly at the stainless steel door in front of you and for no apparent reason start humming the theme song from *Gilligan's Island*.

———•———

One day, while taking the elevator down to the ninth-floor cafeteria, you'll meet a cute African American girl named Becky. Meeting girls in the elevator is difficult because of the no-eye-contact rule, but on this particular day, the elevator will suddenly lose power and come to a screeching halt. You and Becky will be the only two in the car. Despite the fact that you suffer from a subtle case of claustrophobia and will feel like screaming, *"Help!!,"* remain calm and, when the lights and power come right back on, be sure to have an expression on your face that says, "No big deal."

Becky will say, "Holy fuck."

Giggle. Wipe your brow.

Say: "Well, that was disconcerting."

Now it will be her turn to giggle. As she does, take the opportunity to ask for her phone number. The non sequitur approach has often worked for you in the past and this time will prove to be no exception.

With another giggle, she'll say, "Sure, why not. After all, we did nearly die together."

Over the next two weeks, waste a lot of time at work by sending internal instant messages back and forth. Get to know Becky through her roses, hearts, smiles, and angry-looking men with green faces. Notice, however, that you have more to say over IM than you do over thirty-five-cent buffalo wings at the local sports bar. After you sleep with her once, let the relationship fizzle out. It will be more than mutual.

A month later, when you run into her in the elevator, say, "Hey, howzit going?"

She'll say, "Fine. You?"

Stick your hands in your pockets and say, "Oh, fine. Busy. You know."

She'll nod.

Stare blankly at the digital floor indicator. Watch as the red numbers descend rapidly. Clear your throat a couple times.

II

AS A HIGHLY REGARDED ADMIN. ASST. in the multimedia department, you will frequently need to take poster-size electrical schematics to the eighth-floor reproduction center, necessitating a twenty-first-floor elevator bank switcheroo. On one such occasion, you'll actually find yourself in the elevator with none other than the chairman of your firm—a man you've seen on the cover of *Fortune* magazine more often than you've seen in person. He'll have his nose in the heftiest legal document you've ever seen. An Asian American fellow—who must be the chairman's personal assistant—will be standing nearby, carrying the addendums and appendixes. As the elevator zooms from twenty-one to eight, eye Mr. Chairman up and down. Notice his pinstriped suit and white cotton shirt with French cuffs.

Think to yourself: *So this is the big cheese, huh? Nice suit. I wonder if he took advantage of the three-for-$600 sale at Today's Man like I did.*

Consider introducing yourself. After all, it isn't every day you get to ride in an elevator with a man who earns more money a year than you will in a lifetime (and does so without a sneaker endorsement no less).

Decide that Mr. Chairman looks too busy to be interrupted with your lowly rat-a-tat. Stare at the ceiling and begin to calculate how long it would take you to earn the kind of money he's earning. Think: *Let's see. With that big raise, I'll be raking in $1,000 a week, or $52,000 a year. Fifty-two divided into, let's see, right, and carry the one, and, hmm, it would only take me 5,700 years to make $300 million. Cool.*

———•———

At the end of the day, get into the elevator and immediately loosen your tie. Notice and appreciate the more relaxed feeling in the car. Eye contact is now possible. People will be smiling because happy hour has arrived.

Feel free to utilize any one of the following to whomever you meet on your way down: "Did you see the memo on the SRT deal?

What are they? Masochists? Fucking hell, could I use a stiff one."
Or "Yes, well, I think we've got our ducks in a row now. Whaddaya say to a tall one?"

———————•———————

From time to time you'll need to spend an hour or so at the office
over the weekend—usually to abuse the photocopier, making thousands of copies of your latest screenplay, which you'll send off to
agents and producers alike only to be rewarded with the following
form letter:

> *Dear aspiring screenwriter,*
>
> *We are in receipt of your script entitled* <u>Monster Flop.</u> *We
> note, however, that something huge and life altering did not
> occur at the end of the first act and therefore regret to inform
> you of our decision to pass on this otherwise nicely typed and
> handsomely bound script.*

Of course, elevator conduct during weekend hours will vary
dramatically from weekday hours. Farting is not only allowed, but
encouraged. Jumping in the air as the elevator comes to a stop is
always entertaining—creating a mini no-gravity situation. And if
you find yourself with the childlike inclination to do so, you may
also press all the floor buttons just before exiting the car like you
did when visiting your grandparents' condo in south Florida. Just
be sure your firm doesn't employ the often-hard-to-spot elevator
cam before doing so. Should your firm employ the often-hard-to-
spot elevator cam, feel free to switch firms. Remember: Admin.
asst. positions, like the salaries they boast, are a dime a dozen.

HOW TO CATCH A SNOWFLAKE
IN THE MIDDLE OF SUMMER

I

BECOME INCREASINGLY AWARE that certain patterns exist. Patterns involving the ways in which you get in and out of relationships with women. Patterns that you deem unhealthy—or at least that your therapist has deemed unhealthy. The day after your twenty-ninth birthday, decide that this is the year you *will* break the patterns. Decide that this is the year you *will* catch a snowflake—even though you've recently started doubting their existence. A new perspective is needed, you decide. A new approach.

You've heard about speed dating, but that sounds way past your bedtime. You've seen personal ads in *New York* magazine, but they seem way too desperate. A friend will suddenly get engaged to a woman he met on the Internet. He'll call you up and rave about the number of people doing it, the infinite variety of websites, and the ability to list yourself anonymously.

"What do you have to lose?" he'll say.

Mention it to your therapist. She'll think it a good idea. She'll say, "Why not? Everyone's doing it."

Shrug your shoulders. Pretend to be mulling it over when really you've already decided you'll give it a whirl. Go home, crack open a Dr Pepper, and power up the computer.

Start by surfing through hundreds upon hundreds of profiles. This will take the better part of a week. Notice that most if not all of the profiles read something like this:

ABOUT ME: I can't believe I'm doing this!!!!!!!! AHHHH!!!!!! 200 words, huh? Okay, well, here goes: My close friends would describe me as a very close friend. I LOVE to laugh. I like going out. But I'm just as happy staying in. Sometimes, if I'm feeling adventurous, I'll do all three: stay in for a few hours, and then go out for a laugh. I'm considered really really funny, but rather than write something here that's actually funny, I'll just assure you once more how funny I am. For work, I'm an event planner—and I LOVE it! Though I work hard, I play equally as hard. But I don't play hard to get. HA! :-) In my spare time, I like to yadda-yadda with my girlfriends on the phone. I also like spending time with my cat, Fleefluffer (CAT HATERS BE WARNED—STAY AWAY!), and trying new things, like TiVo. I'm considered VERY attractive, as you can see from my photo. Nothing like the rest of the unsightly-looking girls on this site who I'm sure weigh enough to be labeled small shipping hazards . . .

Astonishingly, if you search high and low, exhausting every possible combination of criteria allowed (i.e., between 5' 5" and 5' 5½" with green eyes and little to no facial hair, and living within a three-inch radius of your zip code), you just might happen upon a snowflake. As you remember from kindergarten, no two snowflakes are alike. Each is a unique specimen with no traceable predecessor.

You'll know you've happened upon a snowflake because her profile will be unlike anything you've read before. She'll use words like "thrum" and "pettifogger." She'll talk about bird owners as being "f'ing crazy," (a belief you've long held as gospel). Her picture will reveal an attractive woman with long, buoyant, curly locks, a warm, gracious smile, and expansive, sylphlike appendages. Her deep-set inquisitive eyes will expose the inherent and obvious depth of her character. The glow emanating from her face will reveal her self-proclaimed "cynical optimism."

Don't waste another moment. Hotlist her immediately. Next, send her a tease, a wink, a smile, or whatever's handy—and free of charge. Wait for six weeks while she methodically pores over hundreds of other such winks and e-mails. Wait patiently for another six weeks while she goes out on bad dates with men who will incessantly quote TV shows like *Seinfeld*.

Wait as she suffers through a horrendous date with a man who shows up at her door in a T-shirt—seemingly unaware that it's the middle of March with a light freezing rain falling. He'll do a Fonzie-like maneuver with his umbrella as she opens the door to greet him, causing her some concern.

In the meantime, meet a nice girl at a Yankees game and date her on and off for a couple months while periodically checking back in with the online site to see if your snowflake has written.

At long last, after you and the Yankee have struck out, notice that Snowflake has finally added you to her own hotlist. (Later you'll discover that it was actually her homosexual brother, Brian, who hotlisted you, but never you mind right now.)

Notice that she, too, has illegally yet surreptitiously added her

Yahoo! address to her profile. Waste no time in sending her the following short e-mail:

ok. so we've hotlisted each other. now what?

Wait nervously for her response. A day will pass, perhaps two. Chew off all your fingernails as you check your e-mail account every minute on the minute. Wonder if she hotlisted you by mistake. Perhaps she meant to click on the "remove this loser with the big nose from my account" button, but accidentally clicked on "hotlist big nose" button. Perhaps she's out of town. Perhaps she's been in an auto accident. Make a note to yourself to call all the hospitals in Manhattan and inquire as to whether or not a certain NYChick100023 has been admitted recently.

A few days later she'll write back. It will read:

I think now we call each other. Then maybe get together, and either fall madly in love or decide we cannot stand to be in same room with each other for one minute more.

Along with the note, you'll find her name, Sonja, and her cell phone number. Overjoyed, think about picking up the phone right away but recover at once to avoid looking like a desperate, undersexed, chapped-lipped fellow with foul halitosis. You knew a guy back in junior high who fit that bill. His name was Ken Knot. Recall that Ken, besides being saddled with such an unfortunate name, was fantastically inept when it came to just about anything other than oxygen intake (and even that required the occasional inhaler). Recall how he couldn't even play air guitar well. Bear this in mind as you scribble down Sonja's number and tuck it into your wallet.

Two days later, call her. You'll get her voice mail. Leave a message in your deepest, sexiest voice—something halfway between Howard Stern and James Earl Jones.

Produce a witty line like: "So you're not answering your phone, huh? Have you fallen and can't get up?" Or perhaps something better, but whatever you do, do *not* quote from *Seinfeld*. When she doesn't call back later that night, wonder if she didn't appreciate your sophomoric sense of humor. Or if, perhaps, your James Earl Jones bordered a bit too much on Bea Arthur.

When she finally calls back the next evening, tell her you've just returned home from a softball game and inquire as to whether or not you can call her back after you've had a shower and something to eat. Realize that while not being the most romantic start to a relationship, it's better than telling her the truth: that you're presently beset with wildly painful flatulence from the dried apples you were throwing down your esophagus all afternoon at the office.

Once you've downed some GastroSoothe and feel it's safe to place the call without trumpeting your actual alibi around in the background, dial her digits wistfully. Test your voice a few times while the line rings: "*Eh-hem.* Yes, hi. *Eh-hem.* Hi there, NYChick100023. *Eh-hem.* Hey, howzit going?"

Sadly, you'll get her voice mail.

Curse the dried apples: "Goddamn fucking dried apples!"

Wring your hands in disgust like you saw your dad do once while trying to start the outboard engine on his lemon of a fishing boat. Kick something. Throw an oar.

The apples will rebel by starting their campaign anew. Take action by walking down to the corner Korean deli for some stronger artillery: Imodium's GasAid.

As you're paying for said GasAid, Sonja will of course take the opportunity to call back—causing you to drop change all over the floor as you hastily grope for your cell phone in the pocket of your long shorts.

Grabbing at your side, trying to reduce the bloating manually, and affecting your calmest voice, say, "Oh! Hi! No, I'm just at the Korean, picking up a few things. Can I call you back in a few minutes?"

Detect the Jesus-Christ-is-this-thing-doomed tone in her voice when she says, "Sure."

Wonder if she thought you pretentious for calling the Korean deli, "the Korean." Remember that you heard Aidan on *Sex and the City* call it that once. Wonder if in some childlike way you're still idol-worshipping athletes and Hollywood stars. Make a mental note to bring that up with your therapist later in the week.

By the time you get around to calling her back, it will be late. Like maybe 10 p.m. An older-sounding woman will answer the phone, followed by Sonja: "I've got it, Mom!"

And like that, you'll discover that she lives with her parents out on the south shore of, please god noooo, Long Island. Wonder to yourself why a thirty-year-old woman is living with her parents and lying about her location by using the cunning art of Cell Phone Area Code Deception.

She'll be embarrassed, of course, but will recover nicely, leading with: "Well, you said you were looking for someone who was close to her parents."

Though this scares you, laugh wholeheartedly. Offer your own joke in response. She'll laugh too. Soon you'll both be laughing. *Crack:* The ice is broken.

Go on talking for the next—get this—four and a half hours. Reveal deep dark secrets about yourself and your mother, who used to bite her toenails (and probably still would, were she able to reach them). Likewise, she'll tell you about her stalker experience and how she now suffers from Epstein-Barr. You've heard of Epstein-Barr. Refrain from making the joke about your cousin Lenny Epstein passing the bar. It's a rotten joke anyway.

Learn that she has recently returned from a year abroad, where she was recovering from corporate burnout, and is pursuing her master's in child education at C.W. Post. Be happy that she's somehow, miraculously, lost her Long Island accent. Learn that living with her parents is a cost-saving plan, enabling her to go to school full-time rather than limp along in night school for eternity. Admire her for this. Admire her for her candor. Hell, you could be anybody. A serial killer, a child molester, a Jew-for-Jesus—and here she trusts you.

As the night turns into early morning, you'll both be tired but go on talking nonetheless. You'll laugh more than is lawfully allowed for any given phone conversation with a stranger who lives with her parents on the south shore of, please god noooo, Long Island. Your belly will hurt from laughing (which is infinitely better than what was causing it to hurt some hours ago).

Somehow you'll get on the subject of camel toe. You didn't know what camel toe was until you went to Egypt with your best friend some years ago and saw a real camel toe in person. Now, suddenly, it's an expression that makes you laugh your silent laugh. She'll think it funny too and have you go online and download the song, "Cameltoe" by a group called FannyPack. You'll impress her with your DSL connection that allows you to talk and download the MP3 at the same time.

Periodically, she'll let out this adorable little giggle of a laugh—almost like it's coming out through her teeth rather than her mouth. It will kill you. It will stick with you for weeks.

When she tells you that she has plans for the upcoming weekend, waste no time in asking if she'll meet you tomorrow. She'll sense that you're smitten and agree to meet you, but only if you take the train out to her area code—three numbers you've never dialed, much less visited.

———•———

The next morning at the office, despite that you'll only have had a whopping four hours of sleep, notice that you have more energy than you've had in decades. Your senses will be alive. You'll feel as if a cool breeze is blowing through your hair—as if you just bit into a York Peppermint Patty.

Your boss will be out of town, allowing you to cut out of work early. Go home with the idea of taking a nap before the big date. Unfortunately, having downed three tall lattes at work, your heart will be racing from the caffeine (to say nothing of the excitement of the ensuing date), preventing you from catching even five minutes of sleep.

Try counting sheep. Notice that the sheep all have red splotches on their foreheads like Mikhail Gorbachev. Make a mental note to mention this to your therapist next week.

Put on a nice pair of jeans and a white shirt. Vacillate between tucking it in and wearing it out. In, you look clean-cut—like someone her parents would be happy to meet. Out, combined with your unshaven face (remember her profile: "five o'clock shadow is a plus"), you look a little too MTV. A little too wannabe. Go with it tucked in. (Later, of course, you'll discover that she likes it better untucked, but you'll get bonus points for having revealed your cute rear end.)

Run for the subway to Penn Station. You'll be trying to make the 7:09 p.m. train to Baldwin. Look at your watch. It will be 6:50. On the escalator down to the subway platform, some schmuck will have his nose buried in the newspaper, making it impossible to risk life and limb by running down the escalator steps to catch the train you'll presently hear arriving at the station. Miss the subway by a few seconds. Watch it pull away.

Wring your hands in disgust like your dad with the outboard engine again. Kick something. Throw an oar. Make a note to speak to your therapist about pent-up aggression and genetic inclinations toward hand-wringing.

Finally the next subway will arrive. Make an attempt to read *Sports Illustrated* while on the train but instead let your thoughts drift to Sonja. Try to imagine what she'll look like. After all, you've seen a photo depicting only her upper body. After all, she did say last night that her rump was "a bit large." But you have the following information: she's five-five and 120 pounds. Size up other women on the train. Find one who looks about five-five, lanky, with fairly small breasts. Wonder how on earth she could have a large caboose and still weigh 120 pounds. Decide that it'll be fine. Decide that even if it's large, it's her personality that matters most. So what if she's got a little J.Lo junk in the trunk? You're not shallow. You're bigger than that. So what? Yeah. So what. (Keep telling yourself that.)

Reel out of the subway car like the Tasmanian Devil and literally check a bearded hobbling Hasid against the wall to make the 7:09. Run through the train doors with fifteen seconds to spare and quickly find a window seat next to a woman who looks like Oprah Winfrey before she lost all the weight (and gained it again, and lost it, and gained it, and lost it . . .).

You've never been on the Long Island Rail Road before, but you've heard stories. Yes, you've heard stories. Eye passengers up and down, looking for anyone that resembles Colin Ferguson— the man who, in 1993, shot twenty-five people aboard the 5:33 out of Penn Station. Curiously, Ferguson argued that he had been framed, maintaining that someone had stolen his gun and shot the passengers while he slept. Despite the fact that you haven't slept in what now seems like seven weeks, make every effort to stay awake as the train pulls out and heads off toward, please god noooo, Long Island.

Settle in for the ride. Stare stonily out the window as miles of parking lots, Burger Kings, and Midas muffler stores zoom by. Say to yourself, "So this is Long Island."

Audiate Sonja's little giggle in your inner ear. Your soul will warm at the sound of it. Smile to yourself, knowing that in less than thirty minutes, you'll be meeting the teeth from which the giggle emerges.

Notice the young girls seated around you. They'll look like the same girls you've seen online: plastic clips holding up their hair, Syracuse sweatshirts, French manicures, Walkmans blasting, all the while chatting on their cells with thick LI accents: "He did NOT! (pause) Get OUT of he-ar! (pause) I LOVE THAT!" For a moment, and only a moment, wish that Colin Ferguson would walk in and blow your brains out before reaching Baldwin.

Call Sonja at once. Remark on the great quantity of plastic hair clips.

She'll say, "Welcome to Long Guylin!"

Feel a sense of relief that she, too, can mock the subculture. That she, too, finds much lacking in the view out the window. She'll find it cute that you're coming out to visit her in this "hell-hole." She'll make excuses about living there, about growing up there. And in a moment, none of this will matter.

You won't care that she lives with her parents. You won't care that she lives on Long Island behind the Burger King—somewhere out there, past the Pet Stop. And you won't care that you've thrown caution to the wind by running off to meet a girl you've talked to once on the phone the day before. It will all remind you of simpler, less cynical times. Times when you used to do things like this somewhat regularly. Times when you didn't know from heartache.

Before you were jaded. Before your ex hit you in the face with a flying dish. Before you owned property. Before you had an accountant. Before *Dr. Katz* went off the air. Before you started getting up in the middle of the night to urinate. Before you stopped believing in a soul mate. Before you discovered you were lactose intolerant. Before the Internet.

Agree to be picked up at 8 p.m. downstairs in the center of the station. She'll joke that she's wearing tall Wellington boots and a rain slicker. Laugh. She'll accuse you of laughing easily—at almost everything she says. Laugh again. Then again, don't.

Your best friend Hal will call just before the Baldwin stop. He'll sense the excitement in your voice. Having just recently married, Hal might feel a pang of jealousy as you recount the last twenty-four hours. Make him feel comfortable by announcing that things probably won't work out. 'Cause that's what happens to you. Things just never work out. And lately you've been going through women like multivitamins—one a day, plus iron.

But as you're telling Hal this, feel, perhaps for the first time in years, like you're spewing out complete bullshit. Feel that spark from last night. Reconnect with the very first moment that you felt like this could be something larger than you. Larger than the Internet. Larger than Oprah, still seated to your left.

Internalize your optimism by noting how excited and alive you feel—especially given that you're running on empty. Tell Hal that Colin Ferguson just walked into your car and that you really must be going.

II

AS PLANNED, she'll be standing at the foot of the steep stairwell as you get off the train. You'll see her before she sees you. Wave like you've known her for years—like when you were a little boy being picked up by your grandparents in Florida after you flew solo for the first time. She won't see you at first. Feel like that little boy as you wave again—big and goofy. Smile broadly. Finally noticing you, she'll wave back—a tight, nervous little wave as her smile begins to grow. Your heart will be pounding. She'll be wearing jeans, just like you. Notice that her butt is cute. As a matter of fact, hot by your standards. Think to yourself: *Ding*—Sonja and You: 1. Colin Ferguson: 0.

As you approach her, she'll extend the most elegant hand you've ever seen—long and sinewy, beautiful in its thinness. The complete opposite of all the stumpy potato-picking hands you've held in past relationships. Shake it firmly but softly as you kiss her on the cheek. Your hand in hers will make you feel like you've come home. Like you've arrived. Like you're falling in love.

Within moments the awkwardness of meeting a complete stranger in the parking lot of a train station in the misty fog of early evening will recede as that familiar giggle once again slips out through her teeth and escapes into the thick twilight.

———◆———

She'll drive a Honda Accord. It will remind you of the one you used to own. Remember when you were twenty-one and your father told you not to leave the car unattended in New York City. Everything you owned at the time was in the trunk and piled high on the backseat. You were on your way to Maine for the summer, where you intended to work as a prep chef. You stopped in New York to visit your girlfriend. This was before she cheated on you. Bitch.

Remember how she wanted to check out a certain dress in a certain dress shop in the West Village and asked you to park—leaving the car unattended. Remember how you came back to the car ten minutes later to find the windows broken and all your possessions missing. Remember how upset you were and how much you hated yourself. Remember how, rather astonishingly, the NYPD caught the guy and everything was returned to you except one sock.

Sonja will drive you to Jones Beach. All the while, you'll have an excellent view of her as she rattles on about the restaurant choices. Forced to keep her eyes on the road, she won't be able to look at you for more than a second or two at red lights. This will delight you—put you at ease. Make a mental note to conduct all future blind dates in this manner.

As you approach the beach, there will be a giant obelisk in the middle of the road. You've seen this obelisk before—in photos and such. It's a famous obelisk.

When you comment on it, mispronounce the word thusly: "Hey! There's that famous oh-blisk."

She'll correct you: "oh-be-lisk."

Make like it's no big deal that you didn't know how to pronounce it.

Say: "That too."

————•————

The restaurant will be right on the beach. It will look like a ski lodge were ski lodges made of poured concrete. The carpet will be an uncomfortable greenish brown, like someone vomited split-pea soup all over the place. Sonja will tell you how she worked in this "godforsaken place" for two days back in the summer of ninety-five.

As the hostess leads you to your table, you'll pass members of the waitstaff. Point to Sonja and say: "She used to work here. Remember?"

They'll stare back at you, but Sonja will get a kick out of it. Do it three more times as you pass a few others. By this point,

Sonja will be guffawing—but not because of your stupid joke, rather because you stepped on a stray cherry tomato and it has squirted all over your pant leg.

Notice that the restaurant's AC is broken as the hostess seats you by a thirty-five-foot-high window affording you a magnificent view of three thousand some-odd trash cans that dot the beach. Beyond them you'll almost be able to see the Atlantic Ocean. Despite the vomit carpet and that it's more humid than a steam room in the restaurant, you can't imagine any other place you'd rather be at this moment. Smile at Sonja as you smooth some butter on your dinner roll. Let the smile tell her exactly how you feel.

A waiter will arrive to take your order. Perspiration dripping from his forehead down onto your menu, you'll order the prime rib.

He'll say, "Yeah, I wouldn't. I mean I'm kinda embarrassed to bring the thing out—it's that small."

Order the fail-proof burger and fries.

He'll say, "Good choice."

Sonja will order only a seltzer (cheap date!). While you're waiting for the food, conversation will turn to Sonja's friend Lissie, who she says was "recently run over by a car."

Say: "Run over by a car? Really? Like *run over* run over, or merely hit by a car? 'Cause if you're hit by a car you usually get out of the thing with an air shoe or something. But if you're actually *run* over, you don't usually live to tell about it."

She'll simply stare at you like: *Ding!* Sonja and You: -1.

———•———

The fail-proof burger will arrive looking only slightly more appetizing than the carpet. Grease will be oozing out of the thing, causing the fries to sag and the lettuce to wilt. Since Sonja picked the restaurant, pretend to like it. Smile heartily as you dig in and make yummy noises as you chew.

In the middle of your second bite, she'll excuse herself, saying, "Excuse me, gotta pee. I do this quite often."

Take the opportunity while she's gone to dump most of the burger and all of the fries into the ficus tree behind your table. Use your fork to bury it all under some topsoil.

———•———

After dinner, stroll along the boardwalk. Though it's foggy as all hell and you have difficulty seeing each other, the smell of the sea and the sound of the waves will create a romantic mood. Reminisce about when you were a kid and used to frequent the Atlantic City boardwalk. Tell her about your uncle Irv who used to be a blackjack dealer and looked like Sam the Eagle from *The Muppet Show.*

She'll tell a hilarious tale about the time she and her friend Jan were verbally accosted by a chinless person in Bermuda shorts who, judging by hairstyle and cleavage, could very well have been a woman.

After Sonja finishes the story, be sure to use Jan's name in a sentence in order to begin to remember her friends' names.

Say: "Jan sounds pretty funny." Or "So Jan is your best friend, then?"

She'll give you points for being a good listener. Send the compliment right back by telling her that, in all honesty, she's the best listener you've ever known for less than twenty-four hours. Tell her that as fun as it was laughing on the phone with her last night, the moment you treasure most is when the conversation quieted down and got serious. The way she delicately probed what you deemed your "tragic flaw."

She'll say, "The thing that you don't know is that while you were speaking, I was busy beating my father, Merrill, at Parcheesi."

Stare at her for a moment, unsure whether or not she's being serious, and then, for reasons you'll never figure out for as long as you live, softly break into the following song: *Please allow me to introduce myself, I'm a man of wealth and taste. . . .*

———•———

Ask her about school, about her course load, etc. She'll tell you about an abnormal psychology class she took last semester. Do everything within your power to refrain from saying: "So what was so abnormal about it?" When it leaks out anyway, take comfort in that she's actually laughing at your awful quip. Seize the moment by kissing her passionately on the lips. She'll respond with a little weak-in-the-knees gesture. Grab her tightly and press her body into yours. It should be blissful. If it isn't, you're not on a date with Sonja. Go back to the beginning and start again with the online service.

A few moments after the kiss, you'll both notice a cute little frog jumping around on the boardwalk in front of you. Note the kiss-frog irony, but say nothing to her about it. Tell her that you haven't seen a real frog since your high school days. Follow the frog down the boardwalk in an attempt to pick it up for closer inspection. It will lead you to a stretch of boardwalk completely covered with frogs. All the same size. All jumping around like they've just hatched from some monster-size frog egg. There will be literally thousands of them. The two of you will be simultaneously overwhelmed with horror, curiosity, and mirth.

Wonder if this is the end of the world. The beginning of a plague. Look out over the sea for a streaming trail of white smoke like in the Cecil B. DeMille version of *The Ten Commandments*.

Begin to worry about what would happen if you and Sonja conceived a child. Ponder: *Would it suddenly up and die like the little bald son of Yul Brynner?*

Freaked out by the frogs, head back to the car. She'll drive you to her neighborhood and point out places of interest. Her grade school, the house where she grew up, Midas mufflers.

She'll drive you to a little man-made lake replete with ducks and parked cars with foggy windows. It will remind you of the little man-made lake in New Jersey where you necked with your high school sweetie. Before you know it, and at her suggestion, you'll be in the backseat of the Honda Accord, madly kissing and grinding just like you used to back in high school. It will be the perfect ending to the perfect blind date. From start to finish, the experience will revive you, unjade you, hand you back your virginity on a Midas-gold platter.

When she kisses you good-bye at the train station, know that you have found a snowflake. The pattern has been broken. And know that, whether or not she ever wants to see you again, you will never doubt that snowflakes do indeed exist. Even in the middle of summer.

HOW TO CREATE A DATABASE

I

RECALL, back during your admin. asst. interview, telling your boss that you were familiar with Microsoft Office. Let it come as no surprise, then, when he calls you into his office and requests that you build the multimedia department a fully functional database. Nod your head as he rattles off an index of criteria that will need to go into the database: RBN numbers, TSR numbers, URL, P&L, and Core numbers. IT location, IPTV channels, CES, FID, IBD, HR, PCS, or WAM department classifications. MCR, SCR, OCR, and ECR functionality, encode rates, kill dates, drop-dead dates, vendor IDs, time codes, employee SS numbers, work numbers, cell numbers, home numbers, pager numbers, modem speeds, shirt-sleeve lengths—the list is endless.

Though you've been with the firm for over a year, you have no idea what most of these things are. Continue to nod in feigned understanding as he then tells you he wants it built with Microsoft Access and that he'll need it to "go live" in two weeks.

II

ON YOUR THERAPIST'S COUCH (yes, there is a couch) later that day, calmly explain the situation: You lied during your job interview, you haven't the foggiest idea how to build a database, you don't know what Microsoft Access is, and you wouldn't know your own sleeve length if it were tattooed on your forearm.

She'll look you over and then say, "You look like a thirty-one or thirty-two to me."

Laugh. Your therapist is funny—that's why you stick with her. You may not have learned a thing about yourself over the last year, but the sessions certainly are entertaining.

III

MEET SONJA, the new girl you've been seeing over the last few weeks, for dinner in the meatpacking district. The restaurant will have a definitive southwestern theme going on. Note the cowboy hats, spurs, and gun holsters strewn over the walls. Cringe at the Kenny Rogers tune raining down on you from the recessed ceiling speakers. The waitstaff—biker type (wo?)men with farmer's tans—will be walking around the joint with lassos strung from their belt loops—with biceps ten times the size of your own.

Softly rub Sonja's back and whisper, "Are you sure you want to eat here?"

She'll shoot you a familiar smile, which says, "Yeah, I know what you mean—we could wind up on the house specials menu ourselves," but also suggests that she's too hungry to look for something else.

Your waitress person will come by with tap beers in gigantic translucent cowboy-boot mugs. Sonja will get such a kick out of them that she'll order twelve for a girlfriend's upcoming wedding.

Be pleased that you're finally dating an original mind. Someone who steers clear of the de rigueur gift registry. Someone who didn't get sucked into the *Real World*—who, as a matter of fact, didn't even see one episode. Someone who laments that self-stick postage stamps seem to have completely replaced the self-lick kind—like it's not even an option anymore.

Over jerk chicken sandwiches, tell Sonja what your boss dropped on your plate earlier in the day. Run through the whole shtick once more, including the sleeve length bit.

She'll say: "You look like a thirty-one or thirty-two to me."

Then, with a look of pity, she'll offer to tutor you in Access. She knows the basics and swears that if she can make her way around the application, anyone can.

When it comes to technology, you're most definitely not "anyone." Tell her the story about your ex who once gave you a Palm phone for your twenty-sixth birthday. Explain how you painstakingly entered your most frequently dialed numbers, yet (and no one, not even the Palm salesman, was able to figure this out) no matter who you tried to call, the thing invariably dialed the Moviefone guy. Even when you tried to play bowling, it still called the Moviefone guy.

Then, not wanting to reveal your technologically inept side more than you already have, politely decline her proposition. "Let me monkey around with it a bit, and if I still can't figure it out, well, then maybe."

At this, Sonja will make realistic chimpanzee noises and scratch at her armpit. Laugh and then do the same. This is one of the endearing things that keeps you two together—the tendency to act like zoo animals in public places.

Bathtub-size desserts will be placed in front of you—some kind of cobbler. Only there's so much whipped cream and vanilla ice cream on top, neither of you will be able to discern whether it's peach or rhubarb.

One of you will remark: "No wonder this country is so goddamned overweight." It won't matter who says it because you'll both be thinking it. This is another thing that keeps you together— you're always taking words out of the other's mouth.

Last week, for instance, while walking along Riverside Drive, you started telling her a joke you made up in high school. It was about the D'Angelo brothers who lived up the street, Frank and Ralph—identical twins no one could tell apart. You had finished the setup and were about to get to the punch line when she exclaimed, "*Oh!* Wait! I know, it goes something like this: 'Listen, let me be Ralph with you. Yesterday, I got terribly sick. Franked all over the damn place.'" Her punch line was not only similar to yours, but a notch better.

IV

THE NEXT DAY, fiddle around with Access by typing various "keywords" into the help index. When nothing comes up under keyword "SAVE ME!" go to Barnes & Noble during your lunch break to purchase an *Idiot's* guidebook. Approach the information desk and ask a goateed slacker with a permanent glazed-over look on his face if such a book exists.

With the speed of a turtle missing all four legs, he'll scan through a few pages on his computer screen, only to ask, "What was the name of the book again?"

Though it will be difficult, try not to emphasize the word "Idiot" when answering.

After about thirty minutes, as your lunch break nears its end, he'll look up from the computer screen and proclaim, "Yeah, uh, yeah. We just don't have any in the store. Sorry, dude."

Then he'll ask you if you tried looking online. Tell him that you don't have time to wait for the book to arrive by mail and inquire as to whether or not the Barnes & Noble on the next block has the book in stock. This question will, no doubt, stymie him—calling forth a facial expression that suggests complete brain failure. Regard him with a smile as he scratches his head, eyes returning to the computer monitor.

After a few more minutes, never for a moment lifting his gaze from the screen, he'll rattle off the following:

"There's one copy at 1972 Broadway and three copies at 2289 Broadway and one copy at 600 Fifth Ave. (gulp, scratch head), two at 160 East Fifty-fourth, none at 1280 Lexington Ave., none at 240 East Eighty-sixth, wow, looks like there's nine down at Union Square—dewd, you're so stoked—none at 750 Third Ave., four at 675 Sixth, two at 396 Sixth, none at Astor Place, and one at 106 Court Street."

In a taxi headed to East Fifty-fourth (be sure to hail one with no working AC or, alternatively, one that reeks of curry), call Barnes & Noble just to confirm that they do, indeed, have *The Complete Idiot's Guide to Access.* When they confirm that they do, request that it be placed on hold.

Tell your driver to wait in the "No Stopping or Standing at Any Time" zone and hightail it into the store.

V

BACK AT THE OFFICE, tucking the book neatly under a copy of *Multimedia Today,* use your *Idiot's Guide* to build a beginner's level sample database. The book will walk you through the steps needed to create a pet shop inventory database. It will do so with patience and repetition—as if it were written for an eighty-four-year-old woman suffering from Alzheimer's: "Click on the 'Next' button. Did you click on the 'Next' button? Are you absolutely sure you clicked on the 'Next' button? Because if you didn't click on the 'Next' button, you won't be able to proceed to the next step. If you didn't click on the 'Next' button, do so now."

Surprisingly, you'll discover that you have little interest in knowing exactly how many boxes of Scrumptious Chicken and Cheese Flavored Whisker Lickin's you have in stock. Replace the pet shop data with information on how many agents you've shipped your screenplay to; which ones, to date, have rejected you; and from whom rejection is still pending.

In the middle of all this, your boss will approach the cubicle to inquire about your progress on the database. Hide the Access page by bringing up the minutes from yesterday morning's webcast meeting.

With a false sense of confidence, tell him you're pretty busy with other things at the moment but will have it done on time. Not to worry.

He'll look over the minutes on your screen, all the while fidgeting with the rubber band on his retainer. Pointing at the minutes, he'll say, "This should read: 'Richard Demstead will look into 256 KBS'—not KGB. Let's go, knuckle down. Don't want to find yourself up the creek without a paddle, now, do you?' "

Chuckle at your mistake. Pass it off as a simple typo.

Your boss won't find this nearly as amusing as you do.

VI

IN THE EVENINGS, when you're not out with Sonja, work diligently on your latest screenplay. It'll be loosely based on your relationship with her—the way the two of you met over the Internet; that wonderful first date in, please god nooooooooo, Long Island; and all the chills that came after.

Name your protagonist Drew and call Sonja Marilyn. Marilyn is a good name for your leading lady because it's unusual in this day and age. Since Marilyns are generally in their sixties and practically single-handedly responsible for keeping the margarine business afloat, future movie critics will laud you for bucking the stereotype.

Start jotting down things that happen when you're out with Sonja. Keep these notes in a pocket-size mini-journal that says: "Pocket-size Mini-journal" on the cover. It's permissible to note things like, "Sonja revealed tonight that she's had two ménage à trois in her life. One with another woman and a man, and one with two men." However, do not bother with thoughts like, "In screenplay version, Marilyn will only have one ménage—with Drew and a dental hygienist named Beverly." These details should be obvious and writing them down will only take up much needed space in your pocket-size mini-journal.

———•———

One lazy Saturday afternoon, while walking through the arms and armor exhibit at the Metropolitan Museum of Art, Sonja will notice you writing in your journal. When she doesn't say anything, wonder if the note taking annoys her. Broach the subject and ask her if it does.

She'll say, "Would it annoy you if I did it?"

Think about this for a couple of seconds and then respond with a smile, "Why are you answering my question with another question? You sound like my therapist."

She'll say, "Why shouldn't I answer your question with another question? I'm Jewish, am I not?"

Laugh. Say, "Touché."

She'll duck behind a life-size knight clad in armor and, with a French accent, call out, "Sat wuz nusing. En garde!"

Note all this in the journal. It will make for a wonderful scene in "the sixty-page stretch."

VII

WITH ONLY THREE DAYS LEFT before the go-live date and still hardly a clue as to how to build a working database, decide to take Sonja up on her generous offer. Your agent/screenplay database was nearly successful, but for some unknown reason, every time you looked up a Hollywood agent's address, the addresses were all automatically changed to 801 Chouteau, St. Louis, MO 63164, home of Purina.

Sonja will come by your office on a Saturday afternoon. Jack Hayes, a young, potbellied, prematurely balding guy who works in Philanthropy, will notice the two of you coming in. Not to worry. Jack is on your side. He's seen you at the office on the weekends, using the photocopier for your own purposes, and is always friendly. This is due, in part, to the fact that you once caught him masturbating in the men's room. Ever since, he's been your greatest work ally.

Show Sonja the list of requirements your boss has laid out for you. Watch, spellbound, as her hands fly over the keyboard—entering in categories, subcategories, drop-down lists, forms, reports, "Next" buttons, and if-then statements. Stare, agog, as she changes the background colors, foreground colors, and font colors with special red-green-blue codes to match your firm's "branded" colors. Even though you've supplied her with the branded color chart, refrain from asking her what branded colors are. Let her think you know what they are.

Three quarters of the way through, she'll want you to take her out for some sustenance.

With a gentle yet firm tone of voice, say, "You think? You

don't want to finish this first? Then we could celebrate by going to that Italian place you like."

She'll shoot you a look like "I've been slaving away for five hours—feed me or lose me."

———————•———————

Over falafel sandwiches, notice a slightly forlorn expression on Sonja's face along with some tahini on the side of her cheek. Gesture toward your own cheek, indicating that she has some cleaning to do. In her enervated state, she won't get it all off, leaving a smudge under her nose—making her look not unlike Charlie Chaplin.

Chuckle at this. Worn out, she won't be able to laugh with you. Instead, she'll just rest her head in her hands and let out a deep sigh.

Say: "Hey? Hey now? What is it?"

She'll lift her head from her hands and pass it off as a rough week.

She'll say, "The Epstein-Barr is just knocking me out—much worse than normal."

Go over to her side of the booth and cuddle up next to her. Feel a pang of guilt, as if you're partly responsible.

Gently rub her neck and murmur, "Let's forget the database and go back to my place for a nap. Huh? Whaddaya say?"

She'll look at you with tears welling up in her eyes—like Babar the elephant looked after his mother died. Hold her tight. Let the embrace tell her that you're there for her, that you've been doing research about Epstein-Barr online and are learning how debilitating it can be.

VIII

AS YOU BEGIN to delve deeply into the characters in your new screenplay—tentatively titled *The Taming of the Drew*—from time to time find yourself confusing the real world with the fictitious one. Like last week, for instance, when you and Sonja strolled through SoHo lamenting how every art gallery had been turned into a high-end retail outlet. She wanted to stop at the corner flea market to check out a dress that caught her eye. You, on the other hand, felt like something sweet. So you split up for a while.

Standing in line for water ice, you started jotting notes into your pocket-size mini-journal—something about a scene in which Drew's best friend, Miles, gets thrown in jail for putting up "Models Suck" stickers all over SoHo.

Back at the flea market, Sonja was nowhere to be found. But then you recognized her shoes peeking from under the changing area curtain and accidentally called out, "Marilyn? Is that you?"

Sonja whipped her head out from behind the curtain and, obviously annoyed, said, "Nope, just Sonja. But why don't you wait here for a few days and I'll go see if I can find her."

IX

YOUR BOSS WILL BE mighty impressed with the new multimedia database. He'll invite the entire team up to the cubicle for a group demonstration. Not to worry. You're prepared for this. Sonja has coached you extensively—guiding you through possible questions and tutoring you on the answers. In fact, she spent an hour writing down a script, which you memorized on your subway commutes to and from work.

During the group demo, it will come quite naturally for you to pontificate thusly:

"Of course this is just a beta version of the application. I'd expect you all to have suggestions as you familiarize yourself with the program. There are bound to be errors in the programming code as well—creating a few null expressions and annoying error dialogue boxes. But if you'd please keep an ongoing errata list, that would be helpful in easing this thing into phase two. Of course, getting our ducks in a row here is essential, so first things first—lock down your critical reporting requirements, e-mail them to me, and we'll take it from there."

The database will be such an overwhelming success that your boss will call you into his office the next day and offer you a promotion.

"If you'd like," he'll say, "you can move down to the twenty-eighth floor and work as a producer for the webcast group. You'll have your own office—the whole nine yards."

Along with a significant pay raise, he'll offer you your own business cards printed in the firm's branded colors and three additional personal days a year. Of course, you'll be expected to put in longer hours and work some weekends.

Politely thank your boss but tell him you'll need to think it over. This, of course, will be a flat-out lie, for you wouldn't dream of taking on more responsibility and longer hours.

When you relate the whole story of the database over beers to your best friend Hal—an insurance actuary who can mentally calculate liability risk statistics faster than most people can put together their Thursday night prime-time viewing schedule—he'll say, "So let me get this straight: They give you plenty of time to work on your scripts—sometimes even on the job. They give you a phone to make long distance follow-up calls to agents in Hollywood. They give you your own private fax line and all the paper and supplies you need. Full access to a top-of-the-line photocopier, ten days of vacation a year, plus all your health benefits.

Basically, they're paying you to keep a private office in midtown Manhattan. Who in their right mind would take the promotion? I've got to hand it to you pal, whether you ever produce a successful screenplay or not, at least you'll meet your maker knowing you beat corporate America at their own game. Forget insider trading, forget D and O liability claims, your story is the real story. The story of the little guy battling the ghost in the machine. Drinks on me tonight."

When he's finished, say, "D and what . . . ?"

I

ONE FINE SUMMER DAY many years ago, soon after you entered high school, you and your father drove from Philadelphia to Avalon, New Jersey, where he kept his fishing boat. By this time, your father had sold the old lemon with the dud engine and had moved up to a brand-new thirty-two-foot Carver with dual 125-horsepower inboard/outboard engines. And although he no longer spent hours cursing out the motor, there was still plenty of oar throwing and hand-wringing as he fought incessantly with the automatic winch that would not drop the boat's anchor on cue. Wrestling mightily with the winch, refusing to throw the godforsaken anchor into the water, he was forever drifting into sandbars, tall-grassed marshy banks, and, worst of all, other boats. On these occasions, the oar throwing would often lead to fisticuffs with cigar-smoking men named Vic or Mel, who now had three-foot gaping holes in their boat's starboard galley. Aside from lunch, this was always your favorite part of the day. It was a welcome distraction from the otherwise inanely dull pursuit of catching fish—an activity you found about as interesting as an episode of *The McNeill/Lehrer NewsHour.*

Why your father insisted on your coming along, weekend after weekend, summer after summer, was beyond you. Perhaps he thought that eventually, through sheer osmosis, you, too, would one day wake up at 6:00 a.m. on a Saturday morning, pumping your fists with excitement at the opportunity to sit with the window down in bumper-to-bumper traffic on the Atlantic City Expressway, breathing in gallons of diesel exhaust, to then, at long last, drift along with 38,000 other boats, all fighting for space in a narrow overfished back bay tributary with the great hope of being the one lucky guy who'd fool a stupid fish into hanging himself on a hook. Or perhaps he just wanted company. Whatever the reason, and certainly against your will, you found yourself forever accompanying him on his weekend jaunts just as you found yourself forever being eaten alive by green flies the size of small armadillos.

On this particular fine summer day, the two of you drove along, windows down, with the idea of spending the night in Avalon to avoid the early morning stampede down the expressway. A fellow fishing buddy of your father's had a house in nearby Stone Harbor and was happy to offer his "guest bed" (read: air hockey table) in exchange for a fun-filled day out on the boat with the inoperable anchor winch.

As you neared the Garden State Parkway, which would carry you south to Stone Harbor, traffic suddenly drew to a dead stop. One minute you were breezing along, tapping your foot to "Hotel California" (which, it bears noting, you would hear at least six more times before returning to Philly), and the next, nothing. The Panama Canal was constructed in less time than it took you to move a car length. And the worst part? There didn't seem to be any reason for the congestion. No accident being reported on the radio. No flashing lights up ahead. No toll booth within ten miles. No police sirens wailing in the background. Nothing.

And so the hand-wringing began a day early. "Just our *raza-fraza* luck!" your father barked out the window. "What the *raza-fraza-raza* is going on up there?!" he continued, as a small congregation of snails passed by along the shoulder of the road.

An hour later, with the engine now turned off, your father studied a road map, looking for the nearest alternate route. With his nose a few millimeters from the map, he stared blankly for a few seconds, then violently whipped the thing around forty-five degrees and muttered, "I don't know where the *raza-fraza* we are. Here, see if you can find the expressway on this *raza-fraza-raza-fraza* map." And he shoved the thing in your lap.

But even before you had a chance to look, he had started the engine and was turning off onto the dirt shoulder, following a half dozen other lawless individuals.

"Dad," you cautioned, "what do you think you're doing?"

Not really paying attention to you, he remarked, "Now this is more like it."

Ten minutes later—the windshield covered with dust kicked up by the 4x4 in front of you—your father scuffled with an L-shaped tire iron, leaning on a sticky wheel lug, *raza-fraza*-ing louder than ever as he endeavored to change a flat tire. Evidently, people tossed empty beer bottles out their windows and onto the side of the road, a concept that eluded your father altogether.

You tried to lend a hand, throwing your chicken arms into the lug as well. You even contributed a small *raza* and muted *fraza,* but to no avail. The flat couldn't be fixed. Not until AAA came along, which, given the bumper-to-bumper traffic, ate up most of the day. And as you sat there on the side of the road, watching the other cars crawl by, you mulled over the same question you'd been asking yourself for the last several years:

Why can't anyone in my family fix anything?!

II

ALL THESE YEARS LATER, not much has changed. When it comes to fixing things, your family is still inept. Especially you, who can't figure out how to replace the aging tank ball in your toilet. Yes, you, who hasn't the faintest idea that the catlike racket emanating from the thing is caused by a worn-out toilet flapper.

"How should I know what goes on inside that thing?" you'll retort when Sonja asks why you haven't replaced the tank ball.

"That noise doesn't bug the shit out of you?" she'll ask.

Look at her cluelessly. "What noise?"

———•———

The following weekend she'll return with a new tank ball–flapper contraption and her brother, Brian, and his boyfriend, Larry— each carrying a large bag of groceries. Not only will she fix your toilet tank, she'll also fix dinner for the four of you. An opportunity, she says, for you to get to know the family.

As Brian and Larry peruse your CD collection ("That Linda Ronstadt disk isn't mine, guys, in case you're wondering. A friend left it here by accident."), hover over Sonja as she tinkers in the toilet tank. Feel like a first-year medical student observing quadruple-bypass surgery. Marvel at how one woman can both solve your database troubles and install a toilet tank flapper.

When she's finished, she'll say, "There. No more cats in heat."

Hug her passionately. Plant small kisses on the soft peach fuzz adorning her cheeks. Feel like telling her you love her, but then realize it's way too soon. You don't want to scare her off. Better to wait until she says it first, or until after dinner, whichever comes first.

———————•———————

Over free-range chicken and roasted vegetables, Brian will fill you in on the family gossip. Listen intently as you learn that Grandpa Morris hit upon the brilliant idea to bar-code merchandise at supermarkets first. Only the computer hadn't been invented yet. Seeing as he now lives off his meager pension and social security, he never misses an opportunity to recount the tragedy at family circles, weddings, bar mitzvahs, and the like.

Say things like "huh" and "no kidding" as you discover that Aunt Sarah divorced three times before she found the right person and settled down. Laugh appropriately when Sonja adds, "But it turns out that the *right person* was Aunt Sarah's live-in housekeeper, Cynthia. Anyone mind if I finish off the rutabaga?"

———————•———————

Later, over desert, the conversation will turn to bad breath. Sonja will say that she's careful not to eat onions before she sees you. Tell her you do the same, though the truth is you've never given it any thought before. Breathe into your hand discreetly; wonder if she's trying to tell you something.

Larry will give Brian a hard time about the garlic pizza he's always ordering. It turns him off, he'll explain. He can't get an erection when he smells garlic.

Sonja will say, "TMI, Larry. TMI."

Brian will agree and add, "Yeah, and you know what, Larry? It's just garlic. Get over it. Garlic is edible. People eat it all the time, you know? It's not like it's doody."

———•———

After dinner, just as you're doing the dishes, Sonja will announce that she needs a short nap. Though you'll find the prospect of spending the next hour with two homosexual men you barely know unsettling, nod understandingly. Sonja has clearly hit a wall and is struggling just to keep her head up. Show her to the corner of your apartment where the bed is partitioned off behind a faux Japanese silk screen.

"I'm sorry about conking out on you," she'll say as you tuck her in under the blanket.

Say, "Oh, come on. You fixed the toilet. You fixed dinner, which was *amazing,* by the way. Relax. Take it easy. I'll be right out here with Brian. You need anything, just whisper."

She'll wink at you, smile, and then roll over on her side. Kiss her on the earlobe. She'll smell delicious. You'll find yourself wanting to get busy with her. Refrain. Right now she needs to rest. And besides, you need to finish up the dishes.

———•———

An hour or so later, after Brian has sufficiently embarrassed you by retelling the story about how you and Sonja met (stressing how *he* was the one who found you online—how *he* was the one who hotlisted you), Sonja will emerge from behind the screen, yawning, her body sluggish.

"Napover?" Brian will ask.

"Big-time," Sonja will say as she stretches her legs like a dog just waking from a snooze.

Turning to you, Brian will say, "She's a little groggy after a nap. You'll have to get used to it."

Nod. There could be worse things to get used to (your flatulence, for starters).

"What are you doing, sis?" Brian will ask.

"Fixin' to go make water."

Raise your eyebrows. Say, "Fixin' to wha?"

Brian will explain that ever since she saw the movie *Driving Miss Daisy,* she's been quoting Morgan Freeman's character, referring to having to go to the bathroom as "fixin' to go make water."

Say, "Oh, right," as you chuckle like you knew what it meant all along. And then, with a southern accent (like you actually saw the film), say, "You go ahead and fix to make water, baby. It don't make us no never mind."

———————•———————

Meanwhile, it seems you can fix something. A cup of coffee. And if you don't say so yourself, you make a pretty darn good one.

"This *is* excellent coffee," Larry will say as he sips from his mug.

Smile as if to say, "I told you so."

Talk will switch to the subject of coffee. Tell everyone about your personal favorite: the macchiato. No one will know what you're talking about.

Say, "You know, it's like an espresso with a little dab of steamed milk on the top."

Notice that the word *dab* is not a word you would otherwise use were you not in the company of two homosexual men. Make a mental note to bring this up in therapy.

III

COFFEE WILL PLAY an indispensable role in getting you through the woefully monotonous eight-hour day as an admin. asst. Should you be a tea drinker, or perhaps be allergic to caffeine, it is not advisable to accept an admin. asst. position in the first place. You'd be better off working as an AP photographer on assignment in Chechnya or at some other such job that gets the heart rate up naturally.

Begin the day by drinking your first cup on the subway to work. This you'll have purchased from the Korean deli on your corner. They know you by name there and will make you feel like Norm, from the sitcom *Cheers,* every time you walk in. This is wonderful for good, friendly service, the top story of the morning, and your favorite hazelnut blend. However—and this is the only unfortunate side effect—you might have the *Cheers* theme song stuck in your head for the rest of the morning.

———•———

Your second cup of coffee can be purchased at the firm's cafeteria. This should be done as soon as you arrive at the office, before checking e-mail or voice mail. The cafeteria will have a full assortment of their own freshly brewed generic coffees as well as thermoses full of Starbucks. After you fix your coffee, get a bagel from the rack and place it in the toaster. Try not to let your sleeve dangle over the moving conveyer belt, like that one guy you saw a few months ago—causing a complete evacuation of floors one through eight.

At the checkout line, the always-smiling cashier will say, "Bagel with cream cheese, tall latte?"

Never mind that you've been getting the same bagel with jelly for well over a year—refrain from screaming, "It's me, you fool! The bagel with jelly and tall latte guy!" Simply smile and say, "Un-uh, jelly."

On the elevator ride up to your floor, calculate how much money you've saved by getting jelly instead of cream cheese: *Let's see . . . 300 some-odd bagels times 15 cents' difference, carry*

*the one . . . and that's a whopping $45—nearly six macchiatos.
Cool.*

———————•———————

At about 9:30 a.m., having checked all the sports scores, your
e-mail, voice mail, and perhaps having even returned one or two,
it'll be time for a coffee break. Since you refuse to pay for more
than two cups of coffee a day, coffee break coffees, of which there
can be many—depending on how the screenplay is going (or,
rather, the multimedia department's new org chart is going)—
should be obtained from the complimentary coffee bar down the
hall.

Though 9:30 is the busiest time of day at the coffee machine,
this will not distract the cleaning lady from swabbing down the
machine and restocking the coffee packets. Wonder day in, day
out, why she chooses to tidy up the kitchenette during peak hours.
Let this thought consume you for many minutes as you wait for
her to *get the raza-fraza out of the way!*

In the meantime, make idle chitchat with Bob Jenkins, the VP
of CES Finance: "So, Bob, it looks like we've finally got our ducks
in a row on that sticky W9 situation with Yahoo!, huh?"

When he has little to no idea what you're talking about, realize that Bob Jenkins is actually one of the firm's handymen, not
the VP of CES Finance, as you had originally thought. This, it
suddenly dawns on you, would explain the sizable tool belt that
dangles from his midriff.

With the cleaning woman finally gone, shove your favorite
packet of Torréfaction Espresso Roast into the machine. A minute later, after spurting steam all over the place, your instant
cappuccino will be ready. Take a sip. Ahhhh, it's pretty darn
good. In fact, aside from the generous medical benefits the firm
offers, you consider the complimentary coffee bar the greatest

perk. It's amazing, you've often thought, that they don't include it on the list when sending recruitment teams to Wharton and the like.

IV

YOUR THERAPIST'S WAITING ROOM will have the exact same model coffee machine utilizing the same premeasured packets. Only at your therapist's, one has to insert a dollar bill into the side of the thing to get it to work. That is, unless one knows how to jimmy the front panel open with a penny and trigger it from the inside. Not that you'd be the type of person who'd know about such things. (Amazing, isn't it? You can't fix your toilet tank without hiring a plumber or bringing in your girlfriend, but when it comes to getting something for nothing, you're all about it.)

———•———

Since you've met Sonja, you notice that you have much less to talk about in therapy. Long gone are the days when you'd spend the entire session analyzing relationship patterns that ruled your life. Now you spend most of the session gushing in front of your therapist.

"And she went out and bought plastic shelving and organized my kitchen cupboards. Then the weekend after that we spent an entire afternoon collecting abandoned milk crates and she was able to make sense of the train wreck that is my closet."

"Sounds like a good fit."

"Good? It's perfect. It's a perfect fit. She's perfect."

"Careful of that P word, now. Remember?"

"Well, right. I don't mean she's perfect as in *perfect,* I just mean she's perfect for *me.* Like, for instance, the other night we were looking through photos of me growing up—flipping through old albums—and never, not once, did she make fun of me like my girlfriends did in the past."

"They made fun of you?"

"Yeah, you know: 'Oh my God, you look like a Down syndrome kid!' "

Your therapist will laugh.

"It's not funny!"

"Did you?"

"Yes! I did, kind of. But see Sonja never said anything like that."

"What did she say?"

"She said I looked cute growing up. She said I looked like the kind of kid she'd have had a crush on. And that she wished we had met earlier—like back in high school—because she wishes I could have known her pre-Epstein-Barr."

"Bittersweet."

"Tell me about it."

———•———

You'll begin to wonder whether you still need therapy. If it's worth plunking down the co-pay every week just to rattle on about how good things are—about how even Hal, your most cautious friend, the one who's suffered with you through all the fiery beginnings and endured all the sloppy endings, thinks that Sonja might be "the one." (When you took her out to dinner to meet Hal, she didn't shake his hand and toss off the cliché, "I've heard so much about you!" Instead, she said, "Hal do you do?" And when she saw that he enjoyed her corny pun, she kept it up all evening. "Hal about those Mets?" And when the waiter came: "Hal are the fries here?" And when it was Hal's turn to order: "He'll have the Halibut.")

You'll ask your therapist if patients ever take a hiatus, a break, from therapy, when they feel that they aren't benefiting from it like they used to.

"Why?" she'll question. "Do you feel like we've gone as far as you'd like to go?"

And you'll tell her, with a sense of confidence that surprises even you, that lately you've felt like all you do is talk about how wonderful things are with Sonja. And that the sessions are starting to seem like a waste of time and money. And that perhaps you're cured. Perhaps a person doesn't need to be in therapy for years to find happiness. Perhaps she's fixed you.

"Well, if you are indeed *fixed,*" she'll say, "it certainly wasn't me who did the fixing. It was you."

———•———

But the idea of quitting therapy won't sit well with Sonja. She'll recommend that you stick with it; that therapy is a process and there's no fast track.

"Remember, there are no shortcuts along the path to higher consciousness," she'll argue, quoting the fortune you got with Chinese food last week. And having once told her the story about your father and the flat tire on the way to the Jersey shore, it should come as no surprise when she adds, "Besides, I don't want to see you become your father. I'm sure he's a wonderful man, but, well, you know what I mean. Stick with the therapy. Sit in the slow-moving traffic a while longer. See what that's all about. Okay?"

Look Sonja deeply in the eyes. Feel like you did when you went to Vegas that one time and hit the $1,000 jackpot with your ninth quarter. Wonder if you really deserve someone who has their shit together as she does. Wonder if you've limped through enough horrible relationships to arrive at such an embarrassment of riches. And then, without any thought, break into a song you haven't heard since college:

Maybe I'll win
Saved by zero
Maybe I'll win
Saved by zero.

HOW TO KEEP THE MINUTES
WHILE GIVING AWAY THE HOURS

I

WHAT COULD COMPARE to those long summer days when you were a kid, lazing around the backyard at dusk? Remember how the minutes and hours seemed to move ahead with a speed resembling that of a growing blade of grass? Of course, the older you get, the faster the minutes fly by. Especially when you're pushing thirty and working as a lowly admin. asst. for a financial firm whose day-to-day business you couldn't be more clueless about if you were Spanky from *The Little Rascals*.

A "stock" by your way of thinking is a car that Dale Earnhardt Jr. races down in Daytona. And a "bond"? That's either the special thing you and Sonja have going, or a fantastic secret agent who can barrel down the face of Mount Everest on skis fashioned from plastic kitchen utensils all the while dodging machine-gun fire from a few thousand hooded men on snowmobiles. Of course, "bonds," plural, would be a six-foot-one, 190-pound black man who could probably hit a home run into the San Francisco Bay with a #2 pencil if he tried. "Shares" are condos with soiled wallpaper down in sunny south Florida, while "bears" and "bulls" can mean only one thing: Chicago.

Remember back to the day you interviewed for your job. Remember how you nervously asked your boss if a working knowledge of the industry lingo was a prerequisite. Recall how he smiled and then said, "Ahh, forget about the terminology. Everyone flies by the seat of their pants a little in the beginning. So long as you know what third- and fourth-quarter results are, you'll do fine." And how you were suddenly mollified and happy, yet distinctly curious as to why stodgy old bankers would care so much about late game touchdown statistics. Recall thinking, *Huh, maybe these guys aren't so bad after all.* Besides, you were going to work for the multimedia department, not the fixed income division. You knew all about the media from the compulsory communications course you took back at Penn State. How bad could it be? Minutes were minutes. People would speak about nothing very interesting and you'd write it all down. Recall Shelly from your old ad agency— the fine-figured secretary with the IQ of a water chestnut, who kept the minutes during client meetings. If she could do it, well, then so could you.

But of course the task proved to be infinitely harder than you had suspected. In fact, as far as you're concerned, hitting a home run into the San Francisco Bay with a #2 pencil might be a trifle less difficult.

As for the meetings every Friday at 11:00 a.m., don't be surprised if you find yourself *counting* the minutes more often than keeping them. Because, as it turns out, it's not just a bunch of stodgy old bankers speaking about nothing very interesting—it's a bunch of stodgy old bankers in London, San Francisco, Boston, *and* Japan, connected via something called a Polycom phone, speaking over one another about nothing very interesting. To complicate matters, you'll have to decipher the voices of people you've never met, who must be identified as the "owners" of various "actions" that will then be "bulleted" in the minutes. Trying to discern who said what is like trying to discern what the difference is when your optometrist, Dr. Phuk, puts that gigantic thingamajig around your face and asks, "Is it better like this . . ." *clickity-clickity-click* ". . . or like this?" Only, in Dr. Phuk's office, you've got only two choices; in your weekly conference call, you've got more than two dozen (and some with heavy Japanese accents no less). Add some peripheral background noise from passersby on any one of four speakerphone locations ("Hey, Bob, did you see the memo on the SRT deal? What are they, masochists?!") and a heavyset woman from Meeting Services who likes to play catch with the firm's security dog every Friday at 11:05 a.m. right outside your boss's office, and it's no wonder your minutes look something like this:

- Larry (Garry?) Serling from IBD (IPTV?) will speak to Phil Mc(something Irish) re: upcoming ___?___ convention in ~~Vegas.~~ ~~Dallas.~~ Vegas. (Dallas?)

- Al Tokamachi to cancel the Tokyo IPTV (IBD?) weekly video conference until ~~December (September???) 3rd (30th?)~~ until further notice.

- Somebody in London (with the thickest Cockney accent ever) is to do something completely unintelligible by next Monday.

II

ON THE NIGHT BEFORE one such meeting, the last unofficial night of summer, Sonja will wake you at 2:00 a.m. with a phone call. Groggy as can be, whisper: "Ulf? Ulf? Oh come on, it's not Sunday, is it?"

She'll say, "Aww, sweetie, are you having those Ulf nightmares again?"

Slowly come to you senses, only to learn the bad news: Sonja's grandmother has passed away. In a few hours, she and her parents will be flying to Montreal for the funeral preparations.

This is not unexpected. Her grandmother has been in and out of the hospital for the last several months. You and Sonja have already had the "Are you sure you don't want me to go with you?" conversation a few different times. Each time, the answer has been an emphatic no.

Nevertheless, with a polite knee-jerk demeanor, ask, "Are you sure you don't want me to go with you?"

She'll say, "What? So that both of us can miss out on *The Hours* thing?"

Sonja, a huge Michael Cunningham fan, has been looking forward to the tickets you won in your Joseph Stalin screenwriting class last month. The tickets (sadly won by drawing, not by merit) permit you and a guest into a mediated discussion among Cunningham, author of the book *The Hours;* David Hare, who's written a screen adaptation of the book; and Stephen Daldry, who's in the process of directing the script for an upcoming major Hollywood release of the same name.

Getting up to urinate, say, "Oh, right, *The Hours* thing. Isn't it (*yawwwwn*) next weekend though?"

She won't really hear you as she jabbers away with her mother in the background about something that sounds vaguely "but-I-told-you-to-reserve-bulkhead-seats" related. Take the opportunity to urinate, but do so against the rear of the toilet bowl, so you don't blow your cover.

When she returns her attention to you, she'll say, "I'm sorry, where were we?"

Still half asleep, accidentally flush the toilet, thereby negating your prodigious efforts to urinate on the sly. Hearing the flush, she'll say, "Did you just pee?"

With a hearty chuckle, say, "Noooooo. What, are you kidding me? There was a daddy longlegs in the kitchen who wanted to go for a swim."

III

SADLY, your troubles with minutes don't end with the firm's weekly conference call. Recall, for instance, when you first started seeing your therapist and found the forty-five-minute hour particularly arresting. Remember how you felt like there was a gun to your head, pushing you to speak as quickly as possible. But no matter how quickly you spoke, you still felt like you were racing against an hourglass to get all your thoughts out. A race you would invariably lose.

So you got in the habit of leaving your wristwatch at home on Wednesday afternoons at 6:45 p.m. But that didn't seem to help either. Then, instead of knowing how precious few minutes you had left, you squandered them wondering what time it was.

Your therapist suggested that the two of you *spend* time examining your issues *with* time. But you didn't want to *waste* time so you suggested she *change* the time from forty-five minutes once a week to ninety minutes every other week. That way you could come in relaxed, speak leisurely, follow thoughts to their natural conclusion, and *save* time commuting to and from her downtown office (to say nothing of money on subway fares).

But she wouldn't budge! Imagine that. She was determined

to get you to relax within the confines of the forty-five-minute hour. Like a member of the Third Reich, your therapist was when it came to this issue. And so you had no choice but to give in. But then it dawned on you: You were in therapy to deal with issues, were you not? Wasn't this just as important as everything else? Couldn't this in some indirect way be related to your other issues? Feeling like a failure because all of your friends had done more with their lives by now—again, the proverbial gun to the head—was pretty much the same thing, no? And so, in the end, you couldn't thank your therapist enough for making you aware of the minutes. Even if it did mean shelling out more for the subway.

IV

MEANWHILE, your troubles with the meeting minutes continue. Though you've learned to recognize the voices of two regular participants over in London, the Japanese continue to keep you off balance. Even your boss, the one with the propeller hat on his head, can't tell the difference between Mr. Ota, Mr. Ueno, and Mr. Kasai. He'll continually refer to them as one, cunningly serving up questions in this manner: "So what's the mood over in Asia, gentlemen? Cut to the chase" or "And you guys over there on Japan Standard Time? Are we seeing the forest for the trees?"

Then, once Mr. Ota, Mr. Ueno, or Mr. Kasai reply in what might be a highly intelligible version of the English language were it slowed down about 100 mph, your boss will simply reply, "Uh-huh. Right. I see. Thank you for the quid pro quo, Asia," leaving you with nothing but a naked bullet with a lone question mark by its side.

But none of this creates a problem anywhere near as brutal as the one you'll wind up creating for yourself one day as you accidentally send out your latest screenplay (foxily titled "Webcast Usage Analysis_03") to the entire 11:00 a.m. Friday conference call group rather than the minutes that you so dutifully typed up just minutes before.

Only you won't know you made this terribly embarrassing mistake until your boss sticks his head over your cubicle and says, rather calmly, "I know you probably think your job is as easy as pie. And Lord knows I don't mean to be a flea in your ear, but I think we need to have a little tête-à-tête. That is, if you're not too busy at the moment with *Marilyn!!!!*"

V

THE NEXT DAY, on your way home from work, feeling rather fortunate that you still *have* work, stop into the local supermarket for groceries. While shopping, be sure to keep to your Market Rule Number One by never purchasing more than you can carry in two hands. Never mind that there are handbaskets and pushcarts by the entranceway. That would only make things less difficult, especially when your cell phone rings while standing at the back of a long checkout line.

Even though you've been shopping at this particular market for years, you have no idea where anything is. All the same, be sure to stick to Market Rule Number Two, which states that grocery shopping should last no more than ten minutes. As each and every minute counts, walk briskly around the aisles like a lost child looking for his mother.

Say to yourself, "Wasn't the salsa back here last time?"

If something looks appetizing and is colorfully packaged, take it. Pay no attention to ingredients, only prices. If it's under five dollars and can be cooked in a microwave, take it. All fruit and vegetables—anything that can rot, wither, or shrivel—are to be avoided. When both hands are full, grab at things with your teeth or let them dangle around your neck if you must, just so long as you arrive at the checkout line within ten minutes.

Once you've unloaded your colorfully packaged ensemble onto the conveyor belt, begin thumbing through a four- or five-hundred-page magazine with a fetching Hollywood star like Jennifer Aniston on the cover. As your turn to pay nears, flip more frantically through the magazine for the seventh or eighth time, still in search of the Aniston cover story. Roll your eyes and shake your head in bemusement. Do not bother looking up the cover story page number on the contents page because contents pages in such mammoth periodicals are harder to find than cover stories.

Aggravated and convinced that Aniston is serving as nothing more than a cover model to sell copies, shove the magazine upside down into the wrong rack and articulate, "Credit," louder than necessary.

VI

THE NEXT DAY, on your therapist's couch, after you've talked through your Aniston cover story angst ("I'm telling you, they just put stars like her on the cover to sell more copies! There wasn't one page in the damn thing that said anything about Jennifer Aniston!"), find that, for perhaps the very first time, you have practically nothing to say. Let long, pregnant silences ensue—like when Tony Soprano sits sulking in Dr. Melfi's office on *The Sopranos.*

A clock ticking, somewhere off in the background, will be the only sound. Try not to notice it as you stare nonchalantly at the ivy print wallpaper. Twiddle your thumbs and raise the tip of your nose toward the ceiling to clear the nasal passages a bit. Wonder if, perhaps, the quietness means you're making progress—like shelling out one hundred dollars a week to sit in silence means you've entered into phase two of talk therapy: Analyze the Wall-paper.

Eventually, your therapist will ask, "So how are things going with Sonja?"

Tell her that things are basically fine, though her grandmother just died, and you sort of wish you were invited to the funeral. Tell her that it's a sad time and being cut off doesn't make it any easier.

Another long period of silence will ensue wherein you'll think about what you just said: *I wish I had been invited to a funeral?*

After a few minutes, your therapist will once again break the silence by saying, "Our time's almost up, but are you afraid that Sonja has excluded you for a reason? Or is this more about wanting to be the shoulder for her to cry on?"

Think about this for several hours in the elevator on the way down to the lobby. Wonder what percentage of everything you do is motivated by fear and what percentage is motivated by healthier things, like the desire to have a ménage à trois with Sonja and her best friend, Lissie. Make a mental note to bring this up with your therapist during your next session—that is, if the elevator ever reaches the lobby.

VII

TO AVOID A CRAPPY SEAT, arrive at *The Hours* discussion an hour early. Joseph Stalin and a colleague will be standing near the vegetable spread, stuffing their faces with grape leaves and minicarrots. As you wait for your chance to talk to him about his agent, whom, it should be noted, you still haven't heard back from, think about the invention of the minicarrot. Wonder what that laboratory looked like—various failures strewn about the place: regular-size carrots, wheelbarrow-size carrots, and carrots that were so small you'd need tweezers to eat them. Wonder how long it took to get the size just right.

After several minutes, Stalin's colleague will drip some ranch dressing–type dip down the front of his shirt and excuse himself to the men's room. Take this opportunity to corner Stalin against the far end of the bar.

When he sees you approaching, he'll smile and say, "There he is. The next Billy Wilder."

He'll ask you how things are going, what you're working on, and whether or not you've heard anything positive about your submissions. Bring him up to speed and then broach the subject of his agent. Ask him if he'd mind making a call on your behalf to see if it would help move your script to the top of the slush pile.

Taking long sips from his red wine, he'll hedge a bit, as if you just asked him for thirty million dollars to finance your latest project, but then suddenly acquiesce and say, "Well. Okay. Sure. Send me an e-mail tomorrow. Remind me. I'll see what I can do."

And with that, he'll put his wineglass down on the bar and leave you standing awkwardly by yourself. Swig a beer, eat a few minicarrots, and go to your seat.

Since the last piece of fiction you read was probably *Then Again, Maybe I Won't,* your knowledge of the Cunningham book is only through what Sonja has told you. This is what you know:

- Someone named Virginia Wolf, a bisexual who lived in the 1800s, is writing a book called *Mrs. Dale O'way.* Both Wolf and her protagonist contemplate suicide. Wolf winds up drowning herself while her protagonist lives. (This—you will learn through an extremely embarrassing moment during Q&A at the end of the discussion—has nothing to do with the Hollywood movie starring Elizabeth Taylor called *Who's Afraid of*

Virginia Woolf? Apparently there are two Virginia Wolfs—just as there are two George Bushes.)

- A woman, Laura Brown, is reading *Mrs. Dale O'way* in the 1950s. She courts bisexual curiosity and contemplates suicide as well. She has a son.

- A woman, Clarissa, in 2002 is affectionately called Mrs. Dale O'way by her bisexual former lover and famous author friend, Richard, who, it turns out, is dying of AIDS and is the son of the borderline suicidal woman, Laura, from the 1950s. Richard, like Virginia Wolf, winds up committing suicide—serving as a nice tidy device to bookend the three-part, intricately woven plot structure.

Most of the panel discussion will revolve around this main issue: how to turn such a cheery, uplifting, wispy little novel into a major Hollywood hit while still being true to the source material.

Learn that the screenwriter, David Hare, has tried to stick to the original. Learn that director, Stephen Daldry, has cast Nicole Kidman as the bisexual Virginia Wolf—a stroke of genius as far as you're concerned, guaranteeing big box-office receipts. Armed with this exciting knowledge, decide that Kidman, depending on availability of course, would be perfect for the ménage à trois you're planning in the new screenplay. Make a mental note to bring this up with an agent, should one ever return your phone calls.

VIII

WHEN SONJA RETURNS from Canada, she'll stop at your place on the way home from the airport. She won't be sad, just "tired as fuck." Fetch some orange juice from the fridge and bring it to her as she sprawls out on your sofa. Be mildly concerned that she doesn't seem as happy to see you as you do her after a week apart. Wonder if this thought is fear-based—a recurring insecurity you need to address. Note that wondering like this is becoming something you seem to do more and more often. Now worry about *that* instead of the original concern.

Sonja will say, "So how was *The Hours* thing? Tell me? Tell me?!"

Make a mental note to tell your therapist how anticipating news on *The Hours* thing seemed to bring Sonja to life whereas soft kisses on her neck did not. Brood silently for several seconds.

Go to your desk drawer and get the gift you brought back from the panel discussion for Sonja. Watch her face light up as she reads the inscription on the title page of the book: "For Sonja, sorry to hear about your grandmother's passing. Wish you could have been here with us tonight. Best wishes, Michael Cunningham."

And at this, she will finally begin to cry—big, sloppy, wet tears. Watch her as she puts the book down and smothers you with the biggest hug imaginable. Her tears will begin to soak the front of your T-shirt. Say nothing. Just hold her as she heaves up and down, sobbing like a small child. Realize that she is just now beginning to mourn her grandmother's death. Realize that she is just now, for the first time, through her phlegm, telling you that she loves you.

The hairs on your arms will rise in unison, like a church congregation about to sing "Let Thy Chastening Be in Measure." A chill will sweep over your entire body. Tears will well up in the corners of your eyes. You will feel a slight choke in the throat.

Say: "I love you too" and nothing else. Just hold her.

After a few minutes, she'll gather herself up off you and begin rummaging through her suitcase. Handing a small box to you, she'll say, "Go ahead, open it. It was my grandmother's. I thought it might come in handy for all those minutes you have trouble keeping."

Inside the box will be the smallest Dictaphone you've ever seen—a brilliant idea that had never even crossed your mind. Take Sonja's head in your hands and bring your lips to hers. Let the kiss, salty as it may be, tell her how much the gift means to you.

And as the hours pass and autumn approaches, each day will appear to be shorter by one minute. Daylight, like summer, will begin to disappear with little warning, leaving in its place crisper, cooler nights. And all your troubles with minutes, bulleted or otherwise, will begin to slip away as well—causing you to feel, perhaps for the first time in your life, like you're maturing. Or at the very least like you're learning how to interpret English when spoken by the Japanese head of audio-visual services.

HOW TO PICK AN APPLE
AND OTHER FIVE-LETTER WORDS

I

IN ADDITION TO the already discussed complex system of mirrors you've rigged to keep an eye on your boss, the empty desk in the adjoining cubicle has provided you with months of blissful silence in which to create your hot new Drew and Marilyn screenplay.

But as the famous saying goes, all empty cubicles must eventually be filled with amply bosomed event planners who like to crack gum while dissing their boyfriends in hushed whispers over the phone to girlfriends named Sybil or Anastasia or just plain Girlfren.

When the two of you are introduced by the VP of Executive Services, your new neighbor, Alexis, will extend a hand and, in a volume more appropriate for a crowded bar, cry, "Ohhhhh, I hope ya like Z106!! Othawise ya gonna HATE bein' my neighba! Bah-ha-ha-ha-ha-ha!"

Raise your eyebrows in disbelief. Think to yourself, *Honestly, that* can't *be a real laugh, can it?* When she does it again, begin to contemplate suicide.

———•———

But then there's Sonja—the person who makes all things bearable. When you recount the news of Alexis and how you were forced to suffer through Nelly's "Hot in Herre" four times in one day, she'll make sympathetic puppy-dog eyes and say, "Sounds like someone needs a li'l bit a *eh, eh*—just a li'l bit a *eh, eh.*"

Of course, this is one of the greatest things about being in a committed, loving, monogamous relationship: the frequent sex. (Actually, with her chronic fatigue, perhaps not as frequent as you'd like, but certainly more frequent and more intimate than the great embarrassment that was your sex life just five months ago— so don't even think about complaining.) And with Sonja using birth control pills, you no longer have to deal with what you used to call your Condom Conundrums. (1. Which to buy? Ribbed, studded, extrasensitive, cherry-flavored, lubricated, glow-in-the-dark Scooby-Doo, etc. 2. Did you remember to put one in your wallet? 3. Did you remember to bring your wallet? 4. Did the condom break? 5. Okay, when, exactly, did it break? 6. Well, what do you mean you don't know when it broke?!)

Before Sonja, the forces that governed your sex life revolved around five things—or, perhaps better put, revolved *between* five things. Masturbation was the first thing you did when you got up in the morning and the last thing you did before you turned in at night. It was as much a part of your daily routine as sleep itself. In fact, sometimes, if you woke in the middle of the night and had trouble falling back to sleep, you did it again—to calm you, to relax you, to ease you gently back to slumber. But the frequency with which you masturbated created, of course, all kinds of internal conflicts. For though there was cold hard scientific evidence to the contrary, you still secretly believed that one day—after a particularly sleepless night requiring two or three extra wingdings—you'd wake in the morning, rise to brush your teeth, and find that you could see about as well as Mr. Magoo.

Sonja has, therefore, not only revitalized your heretofore dry (as in your mother's cooking, dry) sex life, but has single-handedly saved you from your own single hand and the inevitable day-to-day reliance on Seeing Eye dogs. As a result, your hands suddenly have tons of free time on their hands.

Put them to use, then, by following up on Sonja's idea to go apple picking in upstate New York. This is a local autumnal tradition you've been meaning to participate in ever since you moved to NYC many years ago. A trip was even planned once with, of all people, Ulf and Nanette, but at the last minute things fell through when Nanette contracted food poisoning and spent the weekend fighting off tedious bouts of diarrhea.

Since then, a long list of excuses has prevented you from going. Though if asked, you'd have trouble coming up with any of them other than "It just seems like something I should do with a girlfriend."

Now that you finally have a girlfriend—who not only says she loves you quite often but, it bears repeating, saved you from certain blindness—the timing couldn't be better to pile into her Honda Accord and spend a warm-in-the-sun-but-chilly-in-the-shade Sunday afternoon picking apples.

II

INVITE SONJA TO spend the night with you in the city. This will be the ninth time you've spent the night together. By now you've gotten used to her frequent middle-of-the-night-trips to the bathroom, while she's grown accustomed to your unrelenting gas passing under the comforter—a fairly even trade-off, by your way of thinking.

This is by far the most uninhibited relationship you've ever had. With your college girlfriend—embarrassingly, your only point of reference—*uninhibited* was naïvely defined as being able to say, "Someone needs to brush."

Wake early in the morning, excited about your trip, only to find a large pest control van double-parked right in front of Sonja's car, causing an unfortunate and lengthy delay. Petulantly lean on the horn for a while and then release it. Do this maybe four times in a row. Though you won't succeed in calling out the owner of the vehicle, you'll at least wake everyone else within a half-mile vicinity, allowing you the temporary release you were looking for.

Meanwhile, Sonja, clearly the brains of the operation, will hit on the brilliant idea to go look for the exterminator. Two or three minutes later she'll return with a short, stocky man who bears an uncanny resemblance to Bob Dylan were Dylan missing his two front teeth.

"Sorry 'bout that," Dylan will say, as he attempts to load an extremely large and, from the looks of it, dangerous canister of poison into the back of his van. "I didn't know anyone would be up this early. You know what I'm sayin'?"

Say nothing at all. Just wait patiently as he wrestles with the unwieldy canister.

"Thing's pretty fuckin' heavy. You know what I'm sayin'?"

Sonja will motion for you to give Dylan a hand—if only to speed the process along.

As your back is breaking from the weight of the canister, say, "This stuff looks pretty toxic. Aren't you afraid it might spill on you or something?"

"Ahh, fuck no. Nothing comes out of these things unless I tell it to. You know what I'm sayin'? Besides, you'd have to eat your motherfuckin' body weight in this shit before it'd kill ya. You know what I'm sayin'?"

Say: "Why, yes, you toothless nincompoop, I do know what you're saying. *Now let's move the raza-fraza-fraza-raza van out of the raza-fraza way before* I *kill you!!*" Actually, don't say that. But think it as you nod along in unspoken accord.

———◆———

Fifteen minutes later, cruising up the West Side Highway in Sonja's Accord, stick your hand out the window and do that rising and falling wave thing against the air current.

Sonja, one hand on the wheel, a wide smile on her face, will look over and say, "Is it me, or did that exterminator look like Bob Dylan?"

———◆———

As you inch along in heavy traffic over the Tappan Zee Bridge, Sonja will attempt to teach you one of her favorite driving games, Mental Jotto. Although you don't have an especial affinity for driving games, sit quietly as she lays out the rules:

1) Think up a five-letter word with no repeating vowels or consonants. Something like *viola* is good, she'll explain, whereas *holly* is not because it has two Ls.

2) Once you have a word, she will try to guess it by submitting a list of her own five-letter words with no repeating vowels or consonants.

3) To each word she offers, you're only to tell her how many letters she has in common with your word. For example, if your word is *viola* and she says, "How many in *alive*?" you say four. (The A, L, I, and V.)

4) "*However!* You must never tell me which letter or let*ters* my word has in common with your word because that," she says enthusiastically, "would take half the fun out of it."

Stare at her in vague disbelief. "This is your idea of *fun*?"

"Come on, dude! Don't be such a stick-in-the-mud. I'm the one who has to do all the work. All you have to do is keep track of your word."

Sure, why not. Anyway, with the traffic what it is, it certainly doesn't look like you're getting to the apple farm before the winter solstice arrives. So what do you have to lose?

Think for a few minutes and then say, "Okay, I have my word."

She'll say, "Good. Now—how many in *viola*?"

Say: "Five."

"What?!"

"You guessed it. That was my word."

"You can't use *that* word!"

"Why not?"

"Because that was the demo word!"

"So? You never said there was a rule about *not* using the demo word."

"Are you that lazy that you can't come up with your own five-letter word?"

Shoot her a menacing smile. Roll your eyes. Start over. Come up with a new five-letter word just to appease her. It's a stupid-ass game as far as you're concerned, but she seems hell-bent on playing, so . . .

"Okay," she'll say, "how many in *viola*?"

"Five."

"What?! What the hell are you doing?"

"I'm sorry, but there are five."

She'll sit, quiet for a moment, just shaking her head back and forth like you've officially failed the Jotto test.

Sit in a puddle of silence and then say, "Aren't we finishing the—"

"THE GAME IS FINISHED!" she'll scream, smiling all the while. "You're a freakin' loser and you know it."

"All right then." Look out the window at the gigantic suspension trusses that support the bridge. Wonder how men build such things.

Quietly, with a tone of indifference, say, "The word was *voilà*, but that's okay. Better luck next time."

Duck out of the way as an empty sixteen-ounce bottle of Pepsi comes sailing toward your head.

III

THE LINE TO ENTER the apple farm will be about the size of Cape Cod. You will wonder if perhaps today is the only day the farm is open all year. As you crawl along with the other cars like legs on a centipede, note the signs posted along the road:

An hour later, a little farther up the road, there will be another sign:

AVAILABLE <u>NOW</u>!!
- Gingergold
- Jonamac
- McIntosh
- Greening
- Cortland
- Macoun
- Mutsu
- Empire
- Red Delicious

Meanwhile, you're still trying to guess her word.

"How many in *house*?"

"Two."

"Okay. Now how the heck am I supposed to know which two?"

"Process of elimination. Just remember that there are two in *house* and go on to your next word."

"Are you kidding me?"

"That's why you should start eliminating letters like I did, remember? How many in *stamp*? How many in *stomp*? How many in *stump*? How many in *slump*? You see?"

Nod your head yes, even though you couldn't be more in the dark if you were still in your mother's womb.

WE STILL HAVE 'EM!!
- Jerseymac
- ~~Pristine~~ (SORRY!!!!!!)
- Sansa
- Paulared

Carry on with the game. Sonja will have guessed two of your words by now, lines and radio. Your third word, idiot, was disqualified because of the double I, a rule you still didn't understand, but whatever.

Now it's your turn to guess her five-letter word. Oh joy.

"How many in *apple*?"

"Can't use it. Double P."

"Oh, right. Sorry. Okay. Hmmm. Oh, I know. How many in *silos*?"

"Two S's! Come on!"

"But they're separated by I-L-O."

"It doesn't matter! Jesus! What if my word had an S?"

"Then you'd say, 'One.' "

"But your word has *two*. Don't you get it? Man alive! How did you get through college?"

Think to yourself, *With a lot of alcohol.*

Take a deep breath. Pop a cheese doodle into your mouth. Wipe your hands on your pant leg and say, "How many in *ball-buster*?"

Look out.

Again the flying Pepsi bottle.

———•———

Around midafternoon, just as you're finally making the turn into the farm itself, there will be yet another sign:

> AVAILABLE STARTING OCT. 1st!!!
> GO GET 'EM!!
> - Idared
> - Rome
> - Fuji
> - Granny Smith
> - Northern Spy

Say: "Gee, there's an awfully big selection of apples at this farm. I had no idea it would be like this."

Sonja will say, "Imagine the wonderful pie we can make with Romes and Cortlands and Macouns all mixed together."

"Don't forget the McIntosh. Those are my favorite."

"Really?" she'll say. "I thought you were more of a PC guy."

"No, that's you. Remember? I don't do Windows."

Though you'll want to laugh your ass off, refrain. Stick with the routine the two of you have developed over the last few weeks by calling out in perfect unison: "Bada-bing-bada-boom!"

Stare out the window for a second. Okay, now laugh your ass off.

———•———

After six, count 'em, *six*, grueling hours on the road, your body rather permanently molded into the shape of a car seat, your turn to drive through the admissions area will finally arrive. Never mind that you could have flown to Disney World and back by now, politely take your clear plastic bags from the cute tanned teenager with the cute blond hair on her arms and proceed to the parking area as you're instructed. As it turns out, the parking area will be the entire farm. Which, by your way of thinking, is rather unfortunate. People should be forced to leave their cars at the entrance and make their way through the groves on foot. Express your annoyance to Sonja as you drive up Mutsu Lane.

Say: "See, there? That couple is trying to pick some Mutsus and we're in their way. As a matter of fact, so is that car over there. And that one as well. Jesus! Look at all the cars, would you? What is it with our drive-through society? Doesn't this bug the shit out of you?"

"What do you want me to do? I've got bigger problems in my life—you know?" And with that, she'll grab a couple of plastic bags from your stash and let herself out of the car.

IV

AS YOU PLUCK a few apples from a Mutsu tree, reflect for a moment on Sonja's moods. Lately, you've been noticing certain patterns. In fact, the more time you spend analyzing multimedia data over at the firm—and the more time you spend getting to know your way around Microsoft Excel—the more aware you've become of Sonja's mood patterns. As you stick another Mutsu in your bag, visualize the following bar graph in your mind's eye:

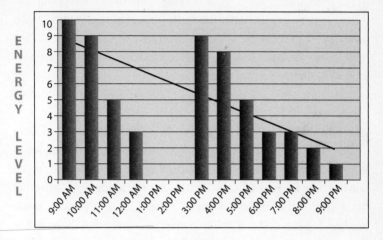

TIME

Notice how she generally wakes at 9:00 a.m. with plenty of energy—on a scale of one to ten, she's usually right around ten. By 11:00 a.m., however, she begins to become irritable as she tires quickly, and her energy drops down to about a five. She always sets aside 1:00–3:00 p.m. for a lengthy nap, unless, of course, you happen to be apple picking, in which case she'll just sit under a Mutsu tree with a flaxseed-filled, lavender-scented eye pillow draped over her face.

When she wakes at about 4:00 p.m., she'll generally do so with renewed energy and can be on for as many as three or four hours in a row. This, you've noticed, is the window most conducive for vigorous games like tennis, squash, or hide the salami.

But by 6:00 p.m. or so, you'll see her once again enervated, putting a bit of a strain on things as you find your own moods following a broad contour around hers—like when she's grumpy and tired, you have no right to feel invigorated or perky.

For instance, you'll want nothing more than to sneak up behind her sitting there under the apple tree as she is now and launch into *"Don't sit under the apple tree with anyone else but me . . ."* but you know you can't, and this puts something of a damper on an otherwise lovely Sunday afternoon.

———•———

Once you've eaten four large Mutsus right off the tree and have filled up two clear plastic bags with dozens more, Sonja will begin to rouse herself back to life. Get back in the car and head out to locate some Fujis or Granny Smiths. Bounce along the bumpy dirt road until you come to Paulared Pass and locate a parking space under what should be, if the little map you received at the entrance is accurate, a Fuji tree. Get out of the car with a couple of plastic bags and begin to hunt for Fujis.

A woman will walk by with her fatigued husband in tow. He'll be pulling two large shopping cart contraptions with dozens upon dozens of bags full of Fujis—like they were the first to arrive this morning and have now picked the grove dry. He'll look like the kind of guy who walks around football stadiums selling #1 fingers for a living.

Go on hunting for Fujis for several minutes before it becomes clear that #1 Finger and his wife *have* picked the entire Fuji grove dry. The only ones left are those rotting on the ground underneath the trees. What's more, as you search from tree to tree, moving deeper and deeper into the Fuji grove, you'll begin to notice Mutsu trees once again—each with plenty of perfectly shaped yellowish-green fruit, ripe for the taking.

Begin to think that you've been suckered into the farm with false advertising. That, while it's true that there are a few trees with other varieties of apples scattered about, the only ones left with pickable fruit are the fucking Mutsus.

Say: "This sucks!" as you kick a rotten Fuji across the grove.

Sonja won't care much, as her picking day is just beginning. She'll yank off a Mutsu the size of a small child's head, take a bite out of it, and say, "So, shall we continue the game?"

Happy that her mood has improved, feign enthusiasm for the game. "Yeah. Sure. Where were we?"

"You were trying to guess my word."

"Ohhh. Right. Okay."

"You should have two of the letters by now."

"That's right," meaning that you agree with her—as in you *should* have two of the letters by now. In reality, however, you probably stand a better chance of finding an unpicked Fuji before discovering even one of her letters.

It's high time you started taking the game seriously. Remember that there were two in *house,* though you still don't know which two. Concentrate. Think of another word that has at least two of the same letters as *house.* This will take the better part of a minute.

"Okay. How many are there in *store?*"

Imitating Groucho Marx with a twig as a cigar, she'll say, "Well, that would depend on the size of the store, now, wouldn't it?"

Amazed that she's the one fooling around now, take the opportunity to up the ante.

Start chasing her around the Fuji grove, screaming, "I'll show you what's in store! Get over here!"

When you catch her, tackle her gently and pin her hands down so she can't move. Kiss her on the lips. Carrying on like an infant, she'll spit the remains of a bite of Mutsu at you. Tickle her. She'll flap with laughter. Kiss her again. Let things get hot and heavy. Begin to make love right there—under a Fuji tree—rolling around on top of a dozen rotten apples.

Sonja will ask, "Are you sure no one can see us?"

Say: "You find me two morons who'd wander this far into an appleless grove."

V

BY THE TIME you're ready to leave the farm, you'll have eaten so many Mutsus that you won't care to pay for the bulging bags you've got in the backseat. As a matter of fact, you won't care if you ever see another apple again, let alone eat one.

Entertain the idea of spilling them out on the path and driving off. It will be your way of getting back at the farm for false advertising. But Sonja, who's by this point tired again, is stuck on the idea of baking an apple pie. Not wanting to rock the boat, pay for the *raza-fraza* apples and offer to drive back to the city. Though she considers you one of the most reckless drivers ever to get behind a steering wheel, she'll have no choice but to hand over the keys. Take them from her, promise you won't zigzag through the dotted lane markers this time, and help her into the passenger's seat.

VI

SOMEWHERE OUTSIDE YONKERS, pull off for dinner. Over barbequed chicken greasier than the Accord's carburetor, watch with amusement as two small children try to win stuffed animals out of the claw machine.

With each attempt and successive failure, one child, the one who just lost his quarter, will look at the other and say, "Aww, man! Didja see that? I had it and then it slipped out! Aww, man!"

Say: "Aren't kids the best?"

Sonya will look up from her pale, shriveled corn on the cob and with a shrug of her shoulders say, "Sure."

See through her words. Realize that she doesn't find children as fascinating as you do.

"That's it? Just, 'sure'?"

"What do you want me to say?"

"I don't know? That yeah, children rock. Or yeah, you can't wait to have your own."

But she won't go there. Instead she'll just stare at you sweetly and say, "Pass me a Wet-Nap, would you?"

Find that her reaction, or more accurately her nonreaction, takes you by surprise. Sort of like when you realized that everybody except you was suddenly walking around town with yoga mats draped over their shoulders.

Hand Sonja a Wet-Nap. Take a bite of potato salad. Turn your attention back to the children.

HOW TO MEET IMPORTANT PEOPLE

I

ONE DAY your boss will poke his head into your cubicle and announce that you've been selected to join a new committee, which he has named the Royal Flush.

The Royal Flush will report directly to his boss, Theresa Royal—one of the firm's managing directors, who works out in San Francisco—and will include five people, as the name implies, from the global multimedia group.

"You'll be the Ten," he'll say, "since you're the youngest."

Happy day.

The face cards will be vice presidents and assistant VPs from all over the world—including the wonderfully unintelligible Mr. Kasai, VP of production in Japan.

Ever since the database success, your boss has been trying to get you more involved with his department's daily operations. Up until now, you've been able to turn down each offer with the same diplomatic mumbo jumbo that got you off the promotion hook. But with this new appointment, your carefree days at the firm will come to an end as a whole host of new responsibilities are added to your job description, including a time-consuming monthly business trip to California.

Your new cubicle neighbor, Alexis, will be the first to congratulate you. "Oh man! That's SO friggin' AUWSOME! Ya must be SOO psyched!"

Force a smile and follow through with the obligatory high five when she prompts you. Begin surfing the Internet for a new admin. asst. position at once.

II

THAT EVENING, you'll have plans to meet Sonja at 6:00 p.m. She wants to see the Broadway production of *Hamlet* before it closes, and a friend of hers said half-price tickets are available at the TKTS booth. You don't like the idea much. Mostly because you equate *Hamlet* with your high school English teacher Dully Dullerbore (actually her name was Dolly Dulabar), who had a monotone voice so utterly lacking in emotional sway and volume, it made the broadcasters on NPR sound like used-car salesmen.

Then there's your problem with TKTS. Every time someone drags you there, you wind up standing in line for hours, listening to some guy play "New York, New York" on steel drums—a musical instrument that never should have been invented—only to get nosebleed tickets conveniently situated behind a theatrical support column. Nevertheless—still surprised that someone like Sonja would be interested in the likes of you—keep your thoughts to yourself and wait patiently in the lobby of your office building, as Sonja will be running late.

When 6:00 p.m. turns into 6:25 p.m., begin to wish one of you had thought to meet in the TKTS line instead. When 6:25 turns into 6:45 and you can't seem to get her on her cell phone, begin to worry that something's wrong. Call her parents' house only to get the machine there as well.

Finally, a little before 7:00, she'll come running into the lobby, her hair an absolute mess. Wonder about that but don't bring it up as the two of you walk briskly down to TKTS.

"I'm sorry," she'll say, slightly winded. "My appointment went late."

Think: *What kind of appointment can mess up hair like that?* But again, don't go there. If nothing else, a year of therapy has at least taught you to give people the benefit of the doubt.

Say: "I hope there'll be good seats left."

"There'll be seats," she'll say.

"Maybe not. It is *Hamlet,* after all."

"Then we'll see something else."

"But you wanted to see *Hamlet.*"

She'll look at you like she is considering clocking you in the face with her shoe, but then smile and say, "There'll be seats."

———•———

When you get to TKTS, find that you're standing in line directly behind none other than Joseph Stalin. He'll look slightly embarrassed because he'll be standing with his agent, who still hasn't gotten back to you about your screenplay.

As you go through the introductions and handshakings, notice that Stalin's agent mumbles to a degree you've never heard before. It will be almost as if he's talking to himself. You won't be sure if he said, "Nice to meet you," or "Mice do eat you."

After some talk about which plays you're hoping to see,

gather the wherewithal to say, "So—I never heard back from you about that script."

As if on cue, Joseph Stalin will look the other way while his agent murmurs, "Script? *Mramra something something* any script."

Get the gist of what he's saying: Stalin never passed your script along. Though you'll want to, don't embarrass your former teacher. Use this opportunity to introduce yourself as an aspiring screenwriter and mention your new script.

Say: "You know what, it's probably for the best. It was my first screenplay, if you know what I mean. Everyone has to get their training wheels, right? The one I'm working on now, however . . ."

Stalin's agent will raise his eyebrows with mild interest as you begin to fill him in. He'll take deep drags from his hand-rolled cigarette and mumble what sounds like "hmmm" and "uh-huh" often. He'll ask questions like, "Who *something mramra* play Marilyn?" and "So *mramra something mramra* in the end?"

Again, only getting the general idea of what he's talking about through context, explain that you haven't given the casting too much thought, other than Nicole Kidman as the lesbian lover. And as for the ending, well, you haven't quite figured that part out yet—but it's bound to be different.

He'll look over at Stalin and mumble, "Jesus, *something mramra* these kids anything in that *mramramra* class? How can he be *something something* through the second act without *mramra something* he's *something or other*?"

Stalin, who evidently speaks Mumble, will come to your rescue: "He *must* have a general sense where he's going with it. After all, he took my course for two semesters, did he not? It's just the particulars that *must* be worked out now. That's how we writers work. It's called planned improvisation." And then looking at you, he'll add, "Isn't that right?"

Steal a glance over at Sonja. She'll have a little smirk on her face. Nod your head with conviction as if you actually *do* have some idea where Marilyn and Drew's relationship is headed. But by this time Stalin's agent will have lost all interest in your story and will change the subject to Jockey underwear—pointing with great enthusiasm to the billboard overhead depicting a man in his briefs with a bulge some two stories high.

———•———

As the ticket line moves forward, prepare to split off from the pack as the TKTS employee directs you to one of the ticket windows. As a parting gesture, Stalin, evidently still harboring guilt over the undelivered script, will invite you and Sonja to an "industry" party next Saturday night in Williamsburg, Brooklyn. Lots of people from the business, including many agents, will be on hand to celebrate the opening of a new soundstage, Stalin says.

"Oh, really? Sure, we'd love to come."

He'll say, "Okay. I'll e-mail you the details."

Smile happily and say, "Wow. Okay! We'll see you there," causing Sonja to kick you hard in the calf.

Once Stalin and his agent are off to their ticket window, ask Sonja what that was all about.

"Gee, I don't know," she'll say with a we're-about-to-have-a-public-row look on her face.

And then it will dawn on you: That's the weekend you're supposed to meet her parents. Saturday dinner, Sunday antiquing trip upstate. Get that awkward feeling in your throat like you just swallowed gum. Close your eyes and let out a deep breath. Wonder how you could have possibly forgotten such an important date. With lightning-fast speed, consider the following reactions:

1) Smack your forehead with an open palm like you used to see your father do in such situations with your mother.

2) Snort up some phlegm (but don't spit it out) and say, *"Oy vey,"* like you used to see your grandfather do in such situations with your grandmother.

3) Smack your forehead, snort up some phlegm, and say, *"Oy vey,"* figuring if #1 got your father off the hook with a woman born in 1946 and #2 got your grandfather off the hook with a woman born in 1914, a combination of the two should work with a woman born in the mid-1970s—if you did the math right.

On second thought, who are you kidding? None of these is appropriate and you know it. Decide to try to get back on her good side with a self-deprecating joke:

"Sorry. Senior moment—seems my memory cells are disappearing faster than Michael Jackson's nose."

———•———

In the theater, watching *Hamlet,* you'll have trouble concentrating on the action. This will be due in part to the—surprise, surprise—partial view. Even if you crane your neck completely to one side, your seat allows you to see only the rear right side of the stage—in other words, the castle moat.

Then there's your stomach, which is up to its old animated tricks again—probably a result of the beef and broccoli you shoveled down five minutes before the curtain went up. Sonja, who may be used to your gastrointestinal problems at home, will sit uncomfortably through most of act two and all of act three with her nose tucked under the front of her shirt. To your ears, Shakespeare's notorious tragedy will sound something like this:

> *Queen:* How now, Ophelia!
> *Ophelia:* How should I your true love know from
> another one? By his cockle hat and staff, and
> his sandal shoon.
> *Sonja:* Again you farted!
> *Queen:* Alas! Sweet lady, what imports this song?

On top of it all, you really want to go to that industry party. So your mind will be busy thinking up ways to meet her parents on Saturday afternoon out in, please god noooo, Long Island, and still be home in time for the party in the evening. It's not that you don't want to meet Sonja's parents—in fact it's something you've been looking forward to for quite some time. But you'd rather not spend the night. When Sonja met your parents, the two of you took the train down to Philadelphia in the morning, had a wonderfully chewy home-cooked meal during which your mother asked Sonja if she wanted another piece of leathery brisket every three minutes, took a lazy stroll around Rittenhouse Square, where your father asked Sonja if she'd like to take some leftover leathery brisket back with her every six minutes, and were back in Manhattan by 10 p.m. Aside from your mother's cooking (why must everything be doused in reconstituted lemon juice?), it was all relatively painless, short, and sweet. What could be better?

III

THE FIRST MEETING of the Royal Flush will take place not in San Francisco, but in New York City. The face cards will fly in from all over the world just to meet one another in person, familiarize themselves with the assignment, and run up hefty tabs at the ritzy W Hotel on their corporate cards. This will make no sense at all because the meeting could have just as easily taken place via video conference, but then again, nothing about the corporate world does. For instance, IT firewalls prevent you from checking your Hotmail account at work because the firm is afraid of contracting viruses. So you give out your work e-mail address to friends, family, and eBay, creating an even greater hazard than without the firewall—brilliant thinking!

———•———

As you sit down with the Royal Flush in conference room 21C, your boss will divvy up the responsibilities. As he does so, notice everyone's taste in neckties. You've seen all these men before, via fuzzy video conferences, but with these meetings, you'll be able to see first hand if each tie fits neatly into your Necktie Theory.

> Hypothesis: *The year in which a man entered the workforce can be ascertained by the pattern and style of his tie. This is especially true of single men who don't have wives or girlfriends to keep their wardrobes up-to-date.*

Take Elliot Stanton from the Boston office, for example. He clearly started working in the early eighties because his tie is exceedingly narrow with an annoying little alligator on it (*definitely* single).

Then there's Lou Silva from the Miami office, who probably got his first job circa 1993. Note that he prefers the black background with wild multicolored patterns on it (again, more than likely single).

Because the old ad agency you worked for didn't require ties, you've started buying them only recently. Between the seven you bought for yourself over the last year and the six you inherited from your father's old collection (only one of which Sonja will let you wear), you're set for the rest of your single days.

Marc Phillips from the London office is a tough call. He's one of these guys who have an extremely bold sense of fashion. For instance, he'll wear a shiny white tie with pink polka dots over a light-yellow checked shirt. Were he not European, he'd most certainly be homosexual. The Necktie Theory doesn't apply to men like him. However, your E-mail Theory, which carries no exemptions, does.

Hypothesis: *A person's standing at the firm is inversely proportional to the manner in which he types his internal e-mail and the amount of words employed.*

For instance, here's an e-mail you might write to Marc Phillips and Lou Silva:

Good morning, gentlemen,

After reading over your proposal for a new recurring conference call on Monday mornings with IT, I can assure you that our team is ready to give the green light so long as you loop back with Carl Tomkins.

Many thanks in advance,

E.M.

And now, the same e-mail written by a vice president:

Gentlemen,

Re: new recurring conference call on Monday morn-

ings with IT—our team is ready to give the green light
so long as you loop back with Tomkins.

Thanks,
VP

And the same e-mail by a senior vice president:

Re: conference call with IT—ready to give green light
so long as you loop back with Tomkins.
SVP

And, lastly, the managing director's e-mail:

fine Just be sure to loop back with Carl

Note how the managing director's sentences have no regard for
punctuation, do away with all salutations completely, and rarely
take up more than one line.

———————•———————

As the meeting draws to a close, realize that you've missed half of
it. Glance at your notes. Aside from the date, the only thing you'll
have written is: *Buy wine!*

Your boss will say, "Okay then. The ball's in your court now.
Make sure each and every one of you has your ducks in a row be-
fore San Francisco." And then, patting you on the back, he'll add:
"Any questions, just ask the Ten."

Do your best to smile and hope that no one notices your face
flush a royal red as you click the cap back onto your pen and rise
to leave.

IV

IN A LIQUOR STORE near Penn Station, pick up a bottle of red wine as a gift for Sonja's parents. Pick up an airplane-size bottle of Dewar's as well to calm your nerves, but at the last minute reshelve it in the wrong place. No one makes a good first impression with liquor on his breath. Leave the store and dash over to Penn Station in the rain. A taxi will hit a puddle, splashing rich brown sludge all over your khakis.

Nice.

Things are off to a good start so far.

———•———

Catch the 1:42 p.m. train to Baldwin. You've done this a few times by now but have never set foot in Sonja's house. She's always picked you up at the train station and hauled you off to the beach.

As you sit looking out the rainy window, once again watching a sea of parking lots and tanning salons fly by, think back to that first date after the marathon phone call. A warm sensation will come over you—like you just walked through a spot in the pool where someone urinated. Shake your head in mild disbelief that you're actually in what your therapist calls "a mature relationship."

Get the urge to tell everyone around you how ecstatic you are that you're happily in love. Overcome with emotions, you'll want to break into song with top hat and cane like the WB frog. Call up Sonja on your cell phone and sing to her:

Hello! ma baby, hello! ma honey, hello! ma ragtime gal

An elderly couple will be sitting across from you. Their glazed-over look will suggest envy, like they're trying to remember what unabashed enthusiasm feels like. Smile at them: *I'm in a mature relationship, folks! Yes-sir-ee! Can you believe it? Me! A mature relationship?!*

"What the hell's gotten into you?" Sonja will ask with a giggle.

"Just excited to see you."

"Awww. Me too. Nervous?"

"A little, yeah. Bought your parents a gift."

"Really? Well that was totally unnecessary, but very sweet."

"I didn't even ask, but I hope they aren't kosher 'cause the wine I got—"

"What?!" she'll scream in your ear.

Realize that you've made a huge mistake but have no idea why. Cautiously say, "What, what?"

"What do you mean, *what* what? You bought wine for my parents when you know my father is in AA? Why would you do that?"

For the next seventeen and a half minutes, the conversation will go something like this:

"You never told me."

"I told you."

"You never told me."

"I told you."

"You did not."

"I did too."

Regard the elderly couple once again with that same glazed-over look on their faces—only now they seem to be the ones talking to you: "Welcome to a mature relationship, son."

———•———

Sonja's parents' house will look exactly how you thought it would. Lots of large framed photomontages on the den walls with early color family photographs slipping out of their mats, some old bowling trophies, a Chanukah menorah with years of wax buildup, an entertainment unit with a lower shelf full of dusty workout videos, a large wood sculpture of Don Quixote and his potbellied sidekick, Sancho Panza, clear Plexiglas bookshelves covered not with books but with small stuffed animals—including a small frog sitting cross-legged with a fishing rod in its hands. And then there will be something on the next shelf that will catch you by surprise: a Japanese soup bowl on which somebody has hand-printed "Miso horny."

Sonja's mother, Jess, a tall, broad woman with a wide streak of gray running down the center of her jet-black hair, will place a vegetable spread on the coffee table and ask you to help yourself and to please call her Jess. Notice the minicarrots and think: *There they are again—damn things are everywhere.*

Her father, Merrill, who insists that you call him by his first name as well, is also tall, but much thinner than Jess—with a pointy Adam's apple that looks like it could kill someone. After you shake his hand and sufficient small talk is made about the torrential rains hitting the region, he'll ask if you'd like a glass of juice or a soda.

He'll say, "Sorry, no alcohol in this house. I'm on the wagon."

Say: "Oh, that's okay, I'm not much of a drinker myself. Haven't been in a liquor store in, gosh, I can't even remember when. Just a Coke, please."

Sonja will shoot you a ha-ha-very-funny look and then announce that you're working on a screenplay, which has several scenes set in Baldwin.

"Is that so?" Merrill will say, bringing you a can of Coke and a glass full of ice. "You know, my father used to be pretty creative with the writing. He once wrote a play about Passover, and everyone in the family played a part."

"Really?"

"I played the part of the youngest child—you know, the one who asks the Four Questions."

Nod your head.

"Oh, it was a wonderful play."

Continue to nod.

"If you want, I can dig it out of the basement. You might enjoy reading it—being as you're a creative type and all."

Jess will throw you a life preserver by interjecting, "Oh, come on, Mer, leave the boy alone—he only just arrived." And then turning to you, she'll ask, "Would you like to see some of our home movies? Sonja in diapers? We just had all ninety-three hours of them transferred from Super-8 to DVD."

———————•———————

Despite the rain, dinner will be served in their screened-in backyard porch. Merrill, evidently the storyteller in the household, will recount the entire family history—from Old World to New—in one gargantuan thirty-minute run-on sentence.

A large purple bug zapper will *zap* incessantly through the course of the meal—each time causing their dog Leila to bark and howl. From where you're sitting, dinner will sound something like this:

MERRILL: . . . and that's when Schlomo came over from Poland you see this was right before the war World War I that is and—

BUG ZAPPER: *ZAAP ZAAAAAP ZAP!!*

LEILA: *Bark! Bark-bark! BARK HOWL!!*

JESS: Leila! Leila! Quiet, girl! Leila!

MERRILL: (not skipping a beat) —he settled in Brooklyn just like Jess's folks did some years later 'course that's a whole other story which perhaps I'll get into after dinner because you see . . .

After dinner, Sonja will announce that she's tired and needs to go upstairs for a little shut-eye. She skipped her usual two-hour nap to be with you, so don't give her a hard time about leaving you alone now with her folks. Just rub her neck softly and nod yes when she asks if you're sure it's all right.

Take a seat in the living room and pick up one of the many family albums Jess has put out for you on the coffee table. Pray that Sonja's parents are like yours in that the father is the designated postdinner dishwasher—because if Merrill comes in and catches you with the album on your lap, you'll most certainly expire before one page has been turned.

"Merrill, honey?" Jess will call from the porch. "Time for you to do the dishes."

Yes!

———————•———————

Sometime later, Jess will come in and sit by your side in the family room. For a few minutes, neither of you will know what to say. Consider the following introductory lines:

1) So, Jess, what did you do for a living before you retired?

2) So, Jess, just how bad is this Epstein-Barr thing?

3) So, Jess, I hear your husband is a recovering alcoholic.

4) So, Jess, is it me, or is your husband a raging windbag?

Let a smile come over your face as you ponder the above lines. But then think: *Ahh, these guys aren't so bad. They're actually kind of cute in their own way. Yeah. Good people. Wouldn't mind having them as in-laws, to be quite honest. Certainly could be a heck of a lot worse. Like my aunt Minerva, for instance. Jesus, is that woman full of hot air. Talk about—*

"So, about sleeping over," Jess will say, interrupting your soliloquy.

"Yes? What about it?"

"Well, with all the rain we've been having, I'm afraid the guest room down in the basement is a bit rancid-smelling. You know, mildewy from the wet floor. Poor Merrill's been up and down those stairs all day—had the sump pump running since the morning—but it's not helping much. Now I know you guys were looking forward to going antiquing with us tomorrow afternoon, but . . . well, I just don't think it's going to happen this time out."

Do your darnedest to affect a melancholic tone: "Oh, wow. That's too bad. Well, I can go back on the train and come out again tomorrow morning, if you guys want."

"Oh, no! Are you kidding? Listen, this rain is supposed to last until Monday, and, well, antiquing isn't much fun in the rain, you know."

"Well, sure. I guess that's true."

V

THE PARTY out in Williamsburg will be winding down when you arrive. This is because Merrill insisted on giving you, get this, a forty-five-minute tour of his garage, which he turned into a lavish workspace after retiring.

Taking each tool out of the custom-built case he made for it, he'd give you it to hold, saying, "Go ahead, take it—feel the weight of that baby."

"No, that's okay, Merrill, really. I've held a drill before."

"But this isn't just any drill! Go on, take it. Squeeze that trigger. Go on."

And so it went with each hammer, screwdriver, and awl. Finally, when he appeared to have finished the tour, you made the mistake of asking what he'd built with all these new tools. Well, that was another half hour at least.

"And over here going down to the basement, I built a new banister for the staircase. Almost cost me the marriage, that one—ha, ha, ha—but she's a beaut, huh?"

———•———

Grab yourself a beer and begin to scan the thinning crowd for Joseph Stalin. When you finally spot him, he'll be making for the exit door. Rush over to him before he leaves and give him a poke on the back.

"Oh," he'll say, "you made it after all."

Explain about the whole meeting of the parents out in, please god noooo, Long Island, and ask if all the important agents have already left.

He'll say, "Important agents? Kid, at your stage of the game, you *must* regard *every* agent as an important agent."

Then he'll ask you if you ever sent anything to the Foster Agency out in Studio City. Even though the name sounds familiar, tell him that it doesn't. He'll point out Ronald Foster over in the corner of the room, chatting with an up-and-coming director. Throw the guilt card and ask Stalin if he'd feel comfortable introducing you. A minute later, find yourself shaking Foster's hand and bidding farewell to Mr. Stalin.

———•———

"Well, that sounds fairly interesting," Foster will say after you've described Marilyn and Drew's relationship. "But where's the twist? A love story like that's gotta have some kind of unusual spin on it—or else it's just another love story."

"What about *When Harry Met Sally*? Where's the big twist there? You know Meg Ryan and Billy Crystal are going to end up together as soon as the movie begins."

He'll stare you in the eyes, either intrigued or amused—it won't be clear—and say, "Are you telling me you've written the next *Harry Met Sally*?"

Look at the floor. Fiddle with the change in your pocket.

"Possibly. It's not done yet."

Instead of giving you his card and asking you to send him the script as soon as you're finished, like you were hoping, he'll merely say, "Well, I've gotta mosey. It sounds promising. Look me up if you're ever in LA. We'll talk."

Watch him walk out the door, coolly waving at some stick-thin pouty-lipped model standing by the entrance. Wonder if he meant what he said about it sounding good. Wonder if anyone in this business ever means what he says. Feel slightly crestfallen as you look around the room. You'll be the last one at the party. Just you and Pouty Lips and a few of the caterers. Wonder what Sonja's up to—what Jess and Merrill are doing this very second. Look at your watch. It will be too late to call.

Get your coat and walk toward the L train. The rain will have stopped. Wonder how the sump pump is doing down in Sonja's basement. Wish you were in that basement now with the mildewy odor and the new banister that almost cost Merrill his marriage.

HOW TO MAKE GOD LAUGH

I

AS AUTUMN BEGINS to cave to the pressure of winter, the view out your therapist's window will start to change. Buildings and neon signs once hidden behind leaves will suddenly appear. The light in her office will grow stark, illuminating cracks in the ceiling that you hadn't noticed up until now.

On this particular day you'll be lying on her couch, staring at the exterior brick façade of an old warehouse across the street. A faded sign stenciled across the entire width of the building will read: "HECKEMER MANUFACTURERS, INC."—probably the company that occupied the building a hundred years ago. It will get you thinking about the transient nature of everything—industry, technology, baseball teams, relationships, seasons . . . shoe fashions.

"Have you noticed that women all over Manhattan are suddenly obsessed with pointy shoes? What's that about? How long will that last? Christ. They look downright painful if you ask me. Ugly as hell too."

Raising her leg to reveal an extremely pointy black shoe, she'll say, "Painful to wear, or painful if you're kicked by one?"

There she goes again. Chuckle cheerfully. Scratch your head. Wonder if you're getting head lice from her pillow.

"Does it scare you?" she'll ask.

"What? Your shoe?"

Now it's her turn to laugh. "No, that everything seems to be so fleeting."

"Sure it does. It scares the shit out of me."

"Are you worried that your relationship with Sonja may be fleeting?"

Take a long time in responding—as if delaying the answer will diminish the fear. Scratch at your ear canal with your pinkie finger. After a good twenty seconds has elapsed: "Yeah. I guess."

She'll take a sip from her coffee mug. "Well, what can you do about it?"

Hedge a bit like you have a lot to say on the subject but only manage an "I don't know."

The truth is, of course, that you do know. Or at least you think you know—but just don't know how to present the plan you've been mulling over for the last couple of weeks to Sonja.

Your therapist won't be satisfied with your answer. She'll continue to probe delicately. "Well, what would the end of this relationship feel like?"

Find that you're not able to answer her. Like that time when your high school girlfriend asked why you prematurely ejaculated.

Blurt out the following instead: "I've got an idea, but I'm not sure how to run it by Sonja. I'm afraid it'll screw everything up."

"What's the idea?"

"Well, see, I'm scared about that too."

"You're scared of the idea?"

"No, of telling you."

"Ahh. You're scared of naming it. You're superstitious."

Let the word *superstitious* hang in the air for a moment.

Say: "Maybe. I don't know. I just keep hearing that old joke in my head."

"What old joke?"

"You know—the old joke about God and the plan."

"Never heard it. How does it go?"

"How do you make God laugh?"

"I don't know, how?"

"Come up with a plan."

"That's cute."

"Cute. Yeah. But true. Haven't you ever noticed? The moment you start hatching a well-thought-out plan—*bang!*—the Big Guy has something else in store for you." The end of your sentence will trail off—drowned out by a noisy fire truck on the street below.

You don't like fire trucks. In fact, you have a serious fear of anything with the word *fire* in it: firehouse, fire alarm, fire drill, getting fired. This probably stems from when you were a small boy and your mother had a matchbook collection. Every now and then you'd take some up to the attic and play. Lighting matches made you feel powerful, grown up, in control—until you set the attic on fire. It was a lot of trauma for a boy your age. Nightmares plagued you for years after.

Your therapist will say, "So let's talk about the big, scary plan then, shall we?"

The big scary plan as you see it: Sonja transfers, say to Hunter College or CUNY—something affordable, but in the city. She moves in with you, still living for free, of course, and finishes up her degree from your place. This way you get to see what living together is like.

"You mean, what living with Epstein-Barr is like?" your therapist will say—not so much as a question but more like a statement.

Think: *Am I that transparent?* Feel guilty—like when you turn off the TV before the game ends because your team is losing.

"Well, yeah. I guess."

Sit in silence. Purse your lips and make this noise: *mwha.* Eventually say, "Is that so terrible? I mean, shouldn't I be worried? Wouldn't you be? A little?"

But your time will run out—the parting, as usual, will be premature. Things will be left unsaid and will have to wait until next week. Emotions and thoughts discarded at the last minute like half-eaten pastries, an ear of corn, or frozen fish found sitting in the candy racks at the supermarket checkout.

II

THE FOLLOWING WEEK, begin to formulate another plan—this one to do with your script. Call Sonja to bounce it off her. Tell her that you're considering dropping in on Ronald Foster next week out in LA to show him your finished script.

She'll say, "*Finished* script? L-A? *Wha?* Have you been sniffing Magic Markers again?"

Tell her that you're going to be in San Francisco next week for the Royal Flush meeting and that you're thinking of flying down to LA after.

"Maybe this is the kick in the rear I need to finish the damn thing."

"A meeting with Stephen Foster?"

Laugh. Stephen Foster wrote songs like "Oh! Susanna."

Say: "So what do you think?"

"Sounds like a decent plan," she'll say, adding, "but I thought you said you couldn't tell whether he was sincere or not. Are you sure it's worth flying to LA?"

Tell her you have nothing to lose—that it's like taking Viagra: You have no place to go but up.

———•———

Spend the next few days wrestling with the end of act three. Think back to your Joseph Stalin class: The protagonist *must* overcome all obstacles in the climax of the film. A ten- to fifteen-minute resolution of the plotlines *must* follow the climax before you fade to black.

This has been the sticking point for the last month or more. Every time you sit down to finish it, you wind up falling asleep on your keyboard only to wake an hour later with three hundred pages that look like this:

;;
;;
;;
;;

It's been worse than writer's block—it's been writer's stroke. If only you knew where your own relationship was headed, it would be simple to resolve things between Marilyn and Drew.

Before Sonja, you'd enter each new relationship and, on the way home from the first date, say to yourself: "Now then—how's this one going to end?"

Because it *was* going to end. They all did. No matter how hard you tried to avoid it, right around the three-month mark one of you would do something completely inane or accuse the other of losing interest or just stop returning phone calls. The details didn't matter much, so long as the relationship sailed straight into the crapper before the ninetieth day.

But that all changed with Sonja. For reasons you still don't understand, things are actually working out—which surprises you even more than when you discovered that hair was suddenly sprouting from your shoulders.

So to finish the script, you'll have to fabricate an ending. In an attempt to create a twist to end all twists, decide to break up Marilyn and Drew on the eve before she's to move in with him. Drew, who will be more than mildly distraught, will lash out by hiring a prostitute. But Drew won't be able to get it up and the prostitute will make off with the precious crystal egg off his mantelpiece— throwing stones at his already wounded soul before the big fade to black.

It's dark, it's different, it's like the noir version of *When Harry Met Sally*. You might even say it's full of Sturm und Drang were you even remotely confident you knew what that meant. But, most important, it's done.

III

WHILE WAITING for your plane to San Francisco, kill some time by wandering around the airport bookstore. You've always been more a magazine guy than a book reader, but lately Sonja has been pushing you to branch out—if for no other reason than to become a better screenwriter.

Pick up several books and read the inside flaps. Most of them will be geared for women and will have titles like *The Shopper, A Shopper Too, The Shopper Takes Manhattan, Revenge of the Shopper, The Girl's Guide to Shopping for a Man*. All of them will have pink-and-white jackets with colorful illustrations of women running or flying to their destinations.

Apparently the bookstore marketing mavericks have noticed trends demonstrating which people buy novels for long plane rides and which buy *Fortune, Sports Illustrated,* and *Rolling Stone.* Feel like you're just another cog in someone named Lester's wet dream of a focus group. Misshelve *Shop Talk III* in the humor section and stroll into self-help. Skim through *Atlas Hugged,* but decide it's not for you.

In nonfiction, the titles will be so long you'll lose interest before even getting to the flap: *A Mind-Blowing, Earth-Shattering, Guaranteed-to-Be-Turned-into-a-Movie Work of Exceptional Testosterone.*

Venture over to young adults—only you won't be able to enter the aisle on account of the new Harry Potter book piled high in every direction. It will be the thickest book you've ever seen. Wonder what it would be like to bench-press a copy. For two seconds only, consider buying a small suitcase at the luggage store across the way and bringing the Harry Potter book on board as your second carry-on.

Be shocked, no, dumbfounded, when you can't find even one book on Henry Ford in the *Auto*biography section. Make a mental note to *register* a complaint with the cashier later. Laugh at your puns. Kill yourself softly with your own song.

Settle on a slim hardcover book from a series called *The Lives and Times of Great Movers and Shakers.* Volume #3 will be about Albert Einstein and Jam Master Jay—two men who have never particularly fascinated you. Buy it anyway, if for no other reason than you like the title: *E=RUN-D.M.C.²*

———•———

On the plane, begin reading about Einstein's life. He played violin in an amateur string quartet. His hair wasn't always that big. He didn't believe God played dice with the universe. Go Fish, maybe, but not dice.

A heavily tattooed man seated next to you will interrupt.

"Einstein, eh?"

"Yup."

Glance at his T-shirt: "Pussy—The Other White Meat."

"Guy was a fuckin' freak. Huh?" Pussy will say, pointing at Einstein's photo on the back of the book.

Shake your head: *Honestly, who's the freak?*

Make the gigantic mistake of asking what line of business he's in.

He'll say, "Ahh, you know—imports mostly. Pharmaceuticals."

Spend the rest of the flight not enjoying your new book, as planned, but listening to Pussy tell you stories about various men he's sent to the hospital. Men who have double-crossed him; men who haven't paid up on debts. Men who have slept with his "hussies."

Your eyebrows, like your tray table, will be locked in their upright position for the remainder of the flight.

IV

CHECK INTO THE HOTEL but before unpacking call Sonja on your cell phone. It will be naptime, her time. Leave a message to let her know you've arrived safely. This was just one of her many instructions when she dropped you off this morning at the airport. Others included: Make sure you don't rent a car with manual transmission and make sure you look up her brother Brian's old lover, Paul.

"What if I forget?"

"Just remember the letter H," she said. "The city is nothing without its hills and homosexuals."

At the Royal Flush meeting, Terry Royal, a powerful-looking woman in her thirties with a large Julia Roberts vein down the center of her forehead, will shake your hand firmly and ask, "And you are?"

"An administrative assistant."

"So what are you doing here?" she'll question.

Just as perplexed as she is, shrug your shoulders and semi-seriously say, "I guess I'm here to make sure everyone has their ducks in a row."

Without a smile, she'll eye you up and down rather suspiciously and then turn on her heel and abruptly ask, "Mr. Kasai, what's the mood over in Asia?"

———•———

The next morning, while waiting for your flight to LA, make several more attempts to get in touch with Sonja. Each time you get her voice mail, hang up. You've already left three messages—any more would cross into the desperate zone.

Begin to feel insecure. Grind your teeth. Stroll over to the coffee shop for the second time in thirty minutes. Release a lot of silent gas along the way and shift into a brisk stride so no one knows who did it.

Back at the gate, try to relax. Remember: You've got to give her the benefit of the doubt. Messy hair or not. Phone call or not. She'll certainly have a good reason, and then, boy, won't you feel like a jerk for letting yourself get carried away with absurd fantasies.

———•———

Land in LA and check into a cheap motel near the airport. Call Sonja again. Voice mail.

Think about calling Jess or Merrill but then decide against it. Too paternal. Too controlling. Her parents will think something's wrong with you. You're beginning to think something's wrong with you. Make a mental note to ask your therapist if she thinks you're starting to lose it.

Call Ronald Foster's office instead.

A nasally female voice will answer. "Foster Agency."

Give your name and tell the woman you're calling for Ronald Foster. Be placed on hold for a minute or so. While on hold, get a call waiting beep in your ear. This will be, of course, Sonja calling at the worst possible time. Think quickly: *Risk losing the Foster call or risk losing Sonja's call?*

Click over to Sonja.

"Sonja?!"

"Hi. How's it going?"

"GoodcanIcallyoubackinoneminute?!!"

"What?"

"JuststaythereI'llcallyourightback!!"

Click back over to Foster only to hear a dial tone. It will be time, once again, to wring your hands in the air and scream obscenities at the top of your lungs. Catch a glimpse of yourself in the mirror as you're doing this. Pretend that you're someone with Tourette's syndrome. Someone like Hal's brother Victor, who was once found wandering around a Kmart parking lot, naked. Scream some more obscenities just because you can.

A gruff voice will be heard from the other side of the wall: "Ahh, pipe the fuck down, ya asshole!"

Take your neighbor's advice. Pipe the fuck down and call Sonja back immediately. You'll get her voice mail. Throw the cell phone at the wall with a velocity that will cause the thing to bust into pieces.

"HEY! FUCKFACE!" your neighbor will boom. "AM I GOING TO HAVE TO COME OVER THERE AND SPELL IT OUT WITH MY FIST OR WHAT?!"

———————•———————

Try to calm yourself by taking a walk outside. At a convenience store pay phone, use your calling card to reach Sonja. Again you'll get her voice mail. Begin to wonder if you're in an episode of *The Twilight Zone.* Look around for Rod Serling.

Though you'll want to, refrain from hanging up on her voice mail again. Leave a message telling her that everything's fine but you'd like to speak to her before you fly home tomorrow. Ask her to call you at the hotel a little later.

———————•———————

Rather than risk embarrassment by calling Foster again, decide it's best to drop in on him at the office. Due to massive congestion on the freeway, the cab ride will cost you an astounding $88.50.

As you fork over the money to your driver in complete disbelief, mutter "*Raza-fraza* traffic! *Raza-fraza-raza* extortion!" under your breath.

Ask for a receipt from the cabbie. Maybe you'll be able to take this as a tax write-off if your script ever sells. If not, you'll at least have proof when you tell everyone the story back home:

"I'm telling you, $88.50 for what should have been a fifteen-minute ride!"

"Come on. You're exaggerating just a little. Admit it."

"The hell I am! Look, here's the receipt!"

———————•———————

Enter the Foster Agency with your script neatly tucked under your arm and approach the nasally voiced receptionist. She'll look exactly like Lucille Ball were Lucille Ball a light-skinned African American woman in her twenties. This will remind you of the rock band you had back in high school named Lucille's Ball. The band practiced every weekend for two years only to lose the celebrated Battle of the Bands because your bassist, Joe Leiter, fell off the stage and broke his collarbone.

Lucille Ball will wonder why you hung up on her. Toy with the idea of telling her the truth but then lie and tell her that your cell phone battery died or you lost the signal or something.

Almost robotically she'll say, "I see. And is Mr. Foster expecting you?"

Recount the story of how you and Foster met. As you're doing this, she'll frequently produce a quiet gum-popping noise out the side of her mouth—though from what you can tell, there's no gum in her mouth.

At the end of your little story say, "So he's not exactly expecting me, but, like I say, he did ask me to look him up if I were ever in town."

She'll just stare at you for what seems like a minute. "I see," adding, "And how long will you be in town?"

Try to introduce some levity: "Well, that all depends on the traffic back to the hotel, now, doesn't it?"

Without a smile, she'll push her glasses up a bit on the bridge of her nose and say, "I see," and then make the gumless cracking noise again.

Then she'll pick up the phone and call into Foster's office. Stand there for a minute, perspiration starting to drip from your underarm onto the script, as Lucille Ball says, "Uh-huh. I see. Uh-huh. I see," over and over again into the receiver.

When she hangs up the phone, she'll return to you: "I'm sorry, but Mr. Foster doesn't have time to meet with you today."

"Well, what about tomorrow morning?"

"I'm afraid not."

Tell her how you flew down from San Francisco just to meet with him—mentioning at least a half-dozen times how he told you to look him up if you were ever in LA. When that doesn't work, try to work the empathy angle by whipping out your taxi receipt and blabbering about the $88.50 and shouldn't that at least buy you five minutes of Foster's time.

"He's a very busy man. I'm sorry," she'll say.

Outraged, say: "So, what then? That's it?"

But as far as Lucille is concerned, the conversation is over. She'll go back to typing some memo—the invisible gum-cracking audible even in the hallway as you wait for the elevator.

V

WALK DEJECTEDLY through a large air-conditioned shopping mall nearby. Begin to doubt not only your future with Sonja but also your future as a screenwriter. Think gloomily about your quickly approaching thirtieth birthday. Let depressing thoughts occupy your mind: You're still working your lowly admin. asst. position at the age of thirty-five—no, forty! Wonder if you even deserve a successful relationship, a successful career. Maybe this is karmic comeuppance for when you were eleven and spent the entire school year making fun of the nerdy kid with the back brace.

Pass a pay phone. Think about calling your therapist for an emergency session. Feel the need to weep uncontrollably—to break down on the pay phone right outside LensCrafters Plus.

"God is SO laughing at me now," you'd croak in between sobbing fits.

Wander aimlessly into a gigantic, sprawling toy store. Pick up a plastic sword and stab yourself in the chest with it. When the blade bends, wish—but only for a second—that it were real. Put the sword back. Stare at a big gumball machine. Wish there were a candy pill you could take to stop you from feeling so sorry for yourself—a PEZ dispenser with sugarcoated Zoloft.

Just then a boy, perhaps four or five years old, will round the corner, bawling his eyes out.

"Mu-mu-mu-mu-mu," he'll say through his snot-covered mouth.

Hold your hand out to him and say, "Whoa. Hey there, big guy. What's the matter?"

"Mu-mu-mu-I can't find-mu-my dad-mu-daddy."

"You can't find your daddy?"

He'll start crying even harder, clutching at a small bag of plastic frogs like a security blanket. Take your shirtsleeve and wipe his face. Tell him that everything's going to be all right—and you'll help him find his father. Slowly he'll calm down as the two of you make your way through the aisles hand in hand. His crying will morph into a little whimpering sound.

"So what's your name?"

"Brian," he'll say. "Brian Silverstein."

"That's a nice name. My girlfriend's brother's named Brian."

"Really?" he'll say, kind of excited, like he didn't know other people might have the same name.

Walk through aisles and aisles of Harry Potter dolls, Harry Potter glasses, Harry Potter wands, hats, board games, rubber balls, action figures, and, your personal favorite, the Harry Potter pottery kit.

In the Teenage Mutant Ninja Turtles aisle, Brian will turn to you. "Wanna see my frogs?"

"Sure." And as he's showing them to you, make a mental note to buy a few bags as a joke gift for Sonja. Begin to devise a plan wherein you're eating at that same split-pea vomit carpet restaurant near the boardwalk where you saw all those frogs. She'll get up to pee and you'll take the opportunity to cover the entire table in plastic frogs.

Stop dead in your tracks. You're doing it again. Cooking up plans.

Brian will say, "What's wrong?"

"Oh, nothing. Just that your frogs scared me a little."

———•———

After an exhaustive ten-minute search for Brian's dad, decide it's time to have him paged. A minute later, Mr. Silverstein will come bounding through the Barbie aisle, a look of sheer panic on his face.

He'll hoist little Brian up into his arms and bark, half relieved, half annoyed, "I told you to wait in the bathroom with me! Jesus, Brian, where did you go?!"

Take a few minutes and fill Mr. Silverstein in on what happened. He'll be so grateful that he'll offer to give you some money. Decline, of course, but agree to an ice-cream cone when Brian begs you relentlessly.

———•———

Over mint chocolate chip sundaes served in plastic cups the size of bicycle helmets learn that Mr. Silverstein is an up-and-coming literary agent looking for edgy scripts from aspiring screenwriters—especially absurd romantic comedies.

Let a huge smile take over your face. Think: *Who has the last laugh now, Big Guy?*

VI

BACK AT THE HOTEL with dollar signs dancing in your head, splurge on an in-room call to Sonja. Your luck will appear to be changing as she picks up on the first ring. Don't even bother with questions about where she's been or why she hasn't kept in touch with you. Get right to the juicy news.

"I think I found an agent!"

"No way!"

"Way!"

"So Mr. Camptown Races do-dahed in the end?"

"No—turns out he *was* the typical superficial Hollywood putz we thought he'd be. But listen to this!"

Be sure to tell the story with all the inherent dramatic irony and then some. In fact, embellish the heck out of it. Tell her Lucille Ball had to call three security guards to have you removed from the premises. Tell her the sword story, but set it in a guns and ammo store. You're an official budding screenwriter now and an agent is considering your script—you've earned such liberties.

When you get to the part about Brian, leave out the frogs, but let the rest of the story unfold exactly as it happened. Tell her how you felt a genuine sense of purpose with Brian gripping your hand like that. And how stepping in to help him made you forget your own problems—trivial by comparison. Tell her how you felt like his foster father for a few minutes and how you were sad to say good-bye to him after the ice-cream shop.

Sonja, who up until the part about Brian was loving every second of the story, will suddenly fall quiet. This will put a slight damper on your enthusiasm.

Say: "Hey? Where'd you go?"

Almost somberly, she'll say, "Nowhere. Was just trying to

concoct a clever foster pun. But I guess I'm too tired to nail one down at the moment. Sorry."

Wonder what it was about the end of the story that tripped her up but try not to let her disposition deflate your excitement. Ah, fuck it. Too late. Like you've suddenly been caught by a powerful undertow, the weight of her mood will drag you down just enough to spoil an otherwise fantastic day.

Hang up the phone. Turn on the TV. There will be a commercial for a compact, travel-size pasta maker. Turn off the TV. Take some of your anger out on the hotel bed by jumping up and down on it repeatedly.

Go across the street to the T.G.I. Friday's for a bowl of pasta. Recall your childhood friend Christoph, whose mother, an Italian immigrant, could never pronounce the word *colander*. Wonder if to this day she still calls it a "spaghetti-stop-water-go-down."

HOW TO ACT PARANOID

I

REMEMBER HOW, during what you now refer to as the Spring-time of Your Therapy, you walked out of each session wondering if you were making progress. Padding along the streets of Greenwich Village, you thought: *I don't feel different. I don't look different. I don't think I'm acting any different. Or maybe I am and the results just aren't perceptible yet. Maybe it's like eating organic food—the benefits of which might only be seen twenty years down the road.*

Fifty-seven forty-five-minute sessions later, come to the conclusion, as you once again assume the familiar position on your therapist's couch, that you are, indeed, making progress. Troublesome disorders and the familiar methods in which you dealt with them are being phased out, conquered, and replaced by newer, more advanced delusions. The fear of success slowly usurped by the fear of being succeeded. The fear of commitment commandeered by the fear of being committed. If this isn't progress—what is?

———•———

"It's just that he seemed so enthusiastic to read it," you'll say, fiddling with a loose button on your shirt. "So to not hear from him yet kind of sucks, you know?"

Your therapist won't answer. By now she knows that you need to spend the first ten minutes of every session gibbering away in a frenzied rant.

"And all that crap with Silverstein is being fueled by the greater paranoia I'm feeling about Sonja—who up until recently was the one stable thing I had going for me. Now—well, now, I don't know. She's been so distant. Something's going on. I'm telling you. Something's *definitely* going on."

And with this, take a deep breath and drape your arm heavily over your eyes. See no more evil, speak no more evil—session rant concluded.

On cue, your therapist will dive right in: "When was the last time you saw her?"

With your arm still covering your eyes, sound forlorn when you say, "When she picked me up at the airport."

"Two weeks ago?"

"Something like that, yeah. Pretty pathetic, huh? So much for asking her to move in with me. Christ. Now I feel lucky when I get a phone call or e-mail from her."

Go back to playing with the loose button.

"What's that like?"

"Phone calls and e-mails?"

"Uh-huh."

"Okay. I guess. You know. Fine."

"Just fine?"

"Well, it just seems like I'm putting a lot of energy and attention into this thing and getting very little back."

"But she's sick."

"She's been sick since we met. I don't buy that. Something has changed. I'm telling you, something has *definitely* changed."

Just like a few years back when you came home from work one day and found Ulf and Nanette doing it in the bathtub. *Your* bathtub—once a safe comforting hideaway almost the size of the rest of your apartment—where you used to lounge under thick steamy clumps of soapy bubbles. But from that day on everything was different. The bathtub was no longer your refuge. It was off limits—a sullied basin—nothing more than a place to put your feet during a quick shower.

"Maybe you're right," your therapist will say. "Maybe something has changed. Maybe her condition is getting worse. Remember what we talked about before? Giving her the benefit of the doubt? Don't forget, *she's* coming into this with a lot of baggage as well. Maybe the stress that intimacy places on a relationship is affecting her physical state. Pushing her buttons. You'll never know until you confront her."

Sit there not knowing what to say. This is how you spend the next ten minutes in therapy—feeling confused, annoyed, guilty, and angry all at the same time. Yank that damn button off your shirt already and shove it in your pocket.

II

SPEND THE NEXT FEW DAYS gathering the courage to confront Sonja. Take long walks through the park, staging mock conversations in your head. Say things like: "I don't have the stomach for this cat-and-mouse shit, honey. There's no reason it needs to be this difficult. Now let's go home and spend the rest of the day making love and lazing around like sea lions." But the problem with mock conversations in your head is that you always give yourself the best lines.

———•———

Meet Hal for a beer and see if you can get him to play Sonja. Discover the problem with this approach is that you can't tell Hal you love him "to the moon and back" without an avalanche of laughter tumbling out of his mouth.

———•———

Go to the movies by yourself. Wish you had even *one* female friend to discuss your problems with. In a concessions line longer than the ticket holders' line, begin to wonder what happened to all your female friends. Sandy from high school: Things pretty much fizzled out after graduation. Cathleen and Beth from college: There, too, things pretty much fizzled out after graduation. Of course, it didn't help that the three of you had a sordid drunken attempt at a threesome—botched on account of your erectile dysfunction. You certainly couldn't look at them the same way after that night.

Other than Hal's wife, a couple of Sonja's friends, and your therapist, the only other woman in your life is Pauline, the sweet chubby girl with the nice smile who works the front desk at the gym. You once overheard her and her coworker giggling because they started getting their periods at the same time. So you said to the coworker, "Periods, shmeriods, Pauline and I have started getting our question marks at the same time." A silly throwaway line, but it made the girls howl with laughter. Ever since, Pauline has treated you like a preferred member—getting your shirts pressed and your shoes polished while you work out even though the entry level membership you pay for doesn't include such luxuries.

———————•———————

Thirty minutes later, *still* in line for popcorn, with your movie about to begin, formulate an open letter to the theater management:

> Dear Mr. Multiplex,
>
> It seems with each passing year you feel the need to add seven new items to your concessions menu. Long gone are the days when small bags of premeasured popcorn lined the display case. Now we have to wait while buckets the same size as the people buying them are laboriously filled to the brim. Long gone are the days when a regular old box of Milk Duds and a beverage of choice sufficed. Now we wait ten hours while pimple-faced teens put cheese on nachos and chilies on hot dogs. As I compose this letter, I'm next in line waiting for the attendant to return to the register. Where did she go, you might ask? To look for cutlery! CUTLERY *in a* raza-fraza *movie theater! What's on board for next year's menu, Mr. Multiplex? Steak and eggs? The traditional date: dinner and a movie, is in danger of becoming extinct, Mr. Multiplex. If you don't reverse current trends soon, my children will grow up saying, "How 'bout tonight we go out for dinner and a dinner?"*

III

KNOWING THAT WATER IS SAID to have a calming effect, take Sonja out for a nice (albeit wildly expensive) dinner at the famous River Café under the Brooklyn Bridge.

Over lobster bisque, bring up the matter as gingerly as possible.

"So where have you been lately?"

"What do you mean?" she'll say, shooing away the waiter as he attempts to refill her water for the seventh time.

"I don't know. Ever since I went to LA, you've been kind of distant."

"Have I?"

Swallow some bisque. Nod yes.

Suddenly a very serious look will come over her face. She'll say, "Look."

Wonderful, here it comes. She's going to dump me in a restaurant I can't even afford. Pass gas under the table.

She'll continue: "I've got to be honest with you."

Nod.

"I don't think I can have children."

Taken by surprise, say, "Excuse me?"

"I know how much you want children, and, well, frankly, I don't think you're going to have them with me."

Take a moment to digést not only the bisque, but what's just been said. Feel at once flattered and frightened that she's thought this far into the future.

Lean in close to her and whisper, "Who said anything about children? And why can't you have them? I don't get it. What's this all about? What's going on?"

She'll explain that she doesn't have enough energy to birth children, let alone raise them. With her Epstein-Barr taking so much out of her, it wouldn't be fair to the children or you. She's discussed this at great length with a specialist. Someone who deals with mothers who have various chronic-fatigue-related afflictions.

Here, she'll start to cry—giving her something of a Goth look as her mascara seeps into her crow's-feet. Have no idea what to say as she blots her tears with her napkin. "I'm sorry" will seem too prescribed. In fact, anything you can think of will seem too prescribed.

You'll want to go over to her side of the table and cuddle up next to her, but it's the River Café, not Pizza Hut. Wait for her to regain composure and then say, "I had no idea."

Sit in complete silence. Listen in on other people's conversations. Wonder who Leonard is and why on earth he'd ever buy anything from the Home Shopping Network. As the main course arrives, affect the pose of an old married couple with nothing to say.

Eventually, she'll look up from her sea bass. "I think you deserve a normal girl. You know, someone you can have a family with."

Shocked and horrified, you'll have two thoughts simultaneously:

1) She's interested in someone else and this is a polite way of easing out of the relationship.

2) The risotto has far too few shrimp for your liking.
   Especially at these prices.

Hear your therapist's voice in your head: *Remember what we talked about before? Giving her the benefit of the doubt?*

With a bemused, slightly blank look on your face, say, "But I love *you*."

She'll start to cry so hard that she'll have to excuse herself to the ladies' room. Move to go after her, but then sit back down—a maneuver you once saw Cary Grant do in some classic film you can never remember the name of. Yeah, that one.

Regard the asparagus on your side dish looking up at you like:

"Here we are! Ready to make your urine smell. Go ahead, take a bite."

Wait several minutes for Sonja to return, all the while wondering if she's telling the truth or not—wondering why relationships have to be so tricky. The truth is, you *do* want children of your own one day. But the other truth is, you really *do* love Sonja, like nothing you've known—and certainly can't imagine spending this much money on food for anyone else.

Take a bite of your asparagus. Break off a piece of bread but then put it back in the basket.

IV

THE NEXT AFTERNOON, call your therapist and book an emergency session. At first she'll say she doesn't have any slots open, but when you mutter *raza-fraza* under your breath, 8:30 p.m. will suddenly free up.

———•———

Sit in your therapist's waiting room. You've never been here this late at night so the view out the window will be one of lights and people cooking dinner in tiny kitchens. It will all seem foreign to you. A familiar room made unfamiliar by the late hour—like when you sat in a grade school classroom with your parents during back-to-school night.

A middle-aged guy will be sitting with his legs crossed and reading *The Hours* in French. He'll be waiting for the therapist next door—the silver-haired woman who, from what you've heard through the wall, conducts her sessions in French.

You studied French in high school and got up to level three, where Pierre went to town to buy groceries. Unfortunately he left his shopping list at home and had to recall everything from memory. When he got home, his wife yelled at him for buying two hundred grams of grain instead of two hundred milligrams. You empathized and wondered how anyone bought food by the metric system.

With an embarrassingly poor accent, turn to *The Hours* guy and say, *"C'est bon livre, non?"*

He'll force a smile like you've just invaded his space and then return his nose to the book. Who said the French aren't friendly?

The Police song "Every Breath You Take" will be on the waiting room radio. Recall an interview you once read with Sting where he said he knew he'd really "made it" when he was laid up in the hospital and overheard the after-hours janitor pushing a mop down the hallway whistling, "Roxanne." Wonder if you'll ever feel like that. Wonder if you'll ever hear back from Silverstein. Wonder if it's time to start devising career contingency plans. Wonder if your after-school job reshelving video boxes at Blockbuster is the closest you'll ever get to show business.

Pull out your pocket-size mini-journal and begin to concoct a lengthy list of jobs that might be fulfilling should you fail to sell your script:

1) ummm???

2)

In therapy, drone on about your dilemma. Break into a cold sweat, feel your stomach quiver. Start to say things like, "I think I'm regressing," but stop midway and pull your hair really hard. Pound your fist into the couch at least three times.

At the end of your rant—today thirty minutes instead of the usual ten—your therapist will say, "So how were things left with her?"

"She said she'd call me soon."

Let your arm fall off your body and land heavily on the floor beside the couch. "Soon. What are we now? Cousins? Soon never means soon. It means anything *but* soon is what it means. Soon. What a load of crap. She's seeing someone. I'm telling you, there's no doubt. She's *definitely* seeing someone."

Your therapist will wait for you to continue. When you don't, she'll say, "Perhaps you're right. Perhaps she is. Perhaps all your paranoia is warranted."

"What? Oh, great! Now I've made a believer out of you too. Jesus. This is bullshit. This is complete bullshit!"

Get your coat and storm out with a lot of hullabaloo. Plod through the waiting room. *The Hours* guy will still be sitting there— now raising his head from his book with a start.

As you pass by, growl: "Richard throws himself out the window in the end. Maybe you should consider the same!"

V

CALL SONJA and tell her you need to speak to her right away. Take a train out to, please god noooo, Long Island. Zoom past parking lots, Midas mufflers, blah, blah, blah.

She'll pick you up in her Honda and drive you to that little lake where the two of you made out in her backseat.

"Remember our first night here?"

"Of course," she'll say, one hand supporting her head against the steering wheel.

"Remember the story I told you about me never crawling?"

She'll look at you with her face scrunched up, all squinty-eyed. "Huh?"

"You know, that I never crawled."

"That must have been the other Internet babe, 'cause you certainly never told me any such thing."

"What are you talking about? We were right here. In the front seat here, at this lake, after the frogs."

Nothing, just an empty stare. And then, finally, "Oh . . . yeah. Right. Tell me again?"

"No, that's it. That's the whole story."

"You never crawled."

"Right. At the age of six months, I just started walking. Grabbed hold of a low-lying windowsill and taught myself to walk."

"Okay, right, right. Now I remember. That's pretty impressive, actually."

"Glad to see the story made such a deep impression."

She'll hit you and say, "Give me a break. Jesus. It was a pretty overwhelming night, you know?"

Begin to tear up. She'll reach over with her long arm and stroke your face gently. Wonder why it is that two people never cry at the same time. It's either one or the other. Like the one who isn't crying has to be there for the other, strong, stoic, supportive. Maybe watching someone else cry builds confidence in some twisted psychological way. Make a note to bring this up with . . . on second thought, forget the note.

"The thing is, a person needs to learn how to crawl. 'Cause life isn't always about walking."

"What are you trying to say?"

Tell her that before LA you were trying to figure out a way for the two of you to live together, which was creating a lot of unnecessary stress. You were jumping ahead when you should have been enjoying what you had. Tell her that you think she's doing the same, now, with the whole children thing.

"I think we need to practice crawling here—forget about baby steps, forget about babies."

She'll run her fingers through her hair and then take off her bra with a lot of commotion, like it's been bugging her for a while. "I just don't think you're going to be happy with me in the long run. You're an athletic guy. You love all those outdoorsy things—baseball, camping, white-water rafting. You know? And that's great. I used to love camping too. But I can't do it. I just can't do it. And you deserve someone who can. Forget about camping—you need someone who doesn't sleep half the fucking day away. And you know you do. So just leave it. You know? Just leave it now before things get . . ."

And now it will be her turn to cry and your turn to comfort. Like a colicky child, she'll go on for what seems like a half hour. But even as you're holding her, continue to be bothered. Think back to the time you were showing her photos from your old album and she remarked that Ulf, who was wearing nothing but boxers, was "fucking hot." Picture her walking on the beach with a tall blond guy, her cell phone strategically turned off, while you hit redial from LAX for the fifty millionth time.

When she stops crying, turn to her and say, "I'm only going to ask this once, and whatever you say, I'll believe you. Okay? Just tell me the truth: Are you seeing someone—you know—on the sly?"

She'll look down at the car seat for a moment and then, without lifting her head up: "Yes, I am."

HOW TO PROLONG A CLIFF-HANGER

HOW TO JUMP THE SHARK

HIS NAME IS Mark Singer. Sonja met him through Lissie, who introduced them at a leukemia fund-raiser at the Waldorf-Astoria a month ago. Since then, Sonja's seen him at least once a week, sometimes more, depending on how she's feeling.

Though you'll be tempted to, do not interrupt her. Remain as cool and collected as possible. Wait for her to finish. When she does, take her hand in yours and sit for a few minutes without saying a word. Listen to an airplane pass overhead. Wish you were on it—flying to Guam, or some such place you have no intention of ever visiting.

It will be a very good thing you remained cool as the following words emerge from her mouth: "So when Dr. Singer—"

Okay, now interrupt. "Dr. Singer?"

"Of course he's a doctor. I told you, Dr. Mark Singer. What did you think?"

Blush. (Don't worry. It will be dark outside; she won't notice.)

Pull this out of your ass: "I thought he was probably a healer or some kind of homeopath. I guess I didn't hear the word *doctor* clearly."

"Oh no," she'll say, "I've already done the holistic thing. Two years ago. What a crock. I had to eat two cloves of raw garlic every morning."

"Sounds harsh."

"Harsh? You should have smelled my breath. Could have melted iron."

Giggle. This is the Sonja you fell in love with. The mood in the car will lighten. She'll say there's much more to tell you but will suggest driving to Friendly's for a coffee and some ice cream before getting into it.

———————— • ————————

One day, when you were a senior in high school, you came home to find your parents waiting for you in the living room. They sat you down and, with hushed voices more suited to a nature program on orangutan mating habits, explained that they were going to try living apart. Difficult as it was for you to hear, it didn't come as a big surprise because the previous summer your father had confessed to having an affair with the girl who serviced his boat down the shore—something that *did* come as a surprise seeing as you never suspected your father as the affair-having type, especially with a woman who wore a "Who Farted?" T-shirt and appeared to be lesbian. The trial separation didn't last, however, and before long everything was swept under the rug and your father moved back home.

But the memory of that day remains and frequently comes up with your therapist, who sees it as part of the root of your inability to trust people.

"This," she says repeatedly, "is why you shudder at the

thought of someone doing something nefarious behind your back."

Your response to this textbook psychobabble: "Show me the person who *does* like someone doing something whateveryousaid behind his back!"

Sitting with Sonja now, as your gaze falls periodically to the exceedingly colorful laminated menu, you can't help but feel exactly like you did that day when your parents spoke in PBS voices.

"When you and I met, I was on something that was developed for the fucking army—for soldiers, to stay awake during combat. Narcoleptics use it," she'll say, making herself laugh even though it's clearly a struggle to talk about.

Though you're having a tough time taking it in, smile along with her—try to make her feel at ease.

As your ice cream arrives, learn that the medication had nasty side effects. Discover that the so-called migraine she had at Hal's pool party back in August was one of many crippling anxiety attacks. Just like the time she excused herself from dinner and spent the next hour in the ladies' room with an upset stomach. Or the time she couldn't meet you after work because her uncle was suddenly in town.

Like in a bad whodunit film, the truth will be revealed slowly, bit by bit, with each sip of coffee. The anxiety attacks worsened. She had to take herself off the narcolepsy medication. She started sleeping through classes and missing others entirely. She was put on Prozac, which made things even worse, and then, finally, just when she actually started contemplating the easy way out, enter Dr. Mark Singer: a psychiatrist who specializes in chronic-fatigue-related afflictions.

"He's the only thing keeping me together," she'll say, rubbing her hand on her cheek as if she's smoothing some cream into her skin.

Stare at her as if you don't know who she is anymore. Wonder if there's more she's not telling you—stuff she'll never tell you for fear of alarming you more than she already has.

"He hasn't prescribed anything?"

"Nope. We just talk—just like you and your shrink, minus the couch. I don't know how I'd cope without him."

Finish your chocolate ice cream but continue to stir the melted part at the bottom of the bowl. Feel hurt that she hasn't included you in any of this. Ask her how—no, *why*—she's kept it from you for so long.

Very matter-of-factly, she'll say, "I loved you. I wanted our relationship to be as normal as possible."

Be bothered by the fact that she's now using the past tense. Shake your head in disbelief. Feel betrayed, lied to, but so sorry for her that your bones hurt.

"So now what?"

She'll look like she's about to lose it. It will surprise you when she doesn't but rather reaches over for your hand and says, "We're stuck, I guess."

"I don't know how you can be so convinced of that when I don't feel the same."

"Because I know you. I know you want children, a normal family: a Volvo station wagon, ski vacations in Telluride. And why shouldn't you? That's what I wanted a few years ago too."

Mull this over as you fiddle with a packet of sugar. Notice your face is warm to the touch. Close your eyes for long intervals—groping for something, anything, to say in return.

Begin to respond: "I just don't feel . . ." but then stop and instead say, "And what if you're wrong? What then? What if I don't want children? You know? What if you begin to get better? What if there's suddenly a cure for Epstein-Barr? I'm not getting this defeatist attitude you're pushing around. You're really ready to give up? Aren't you just going to have the same problem with the next guy you meet? And the guy after that? And the guy after that?"

"Look," she'll say—now with a little edge to her voice, "you can sit there all night long and tell me you might not want children. And yeah, maybe you could even convince yourself of that now—God knows it's hard to find someone who just gets it, who gets you. But five, ten years down the road you *are* going to want children. And then what? Then you're going to resent me. You're going to wind up holding this over my head. And if not this then something else. And yeah, maybe they'll find a cure in the meantime. But you know what? I can't live for the meantime. You don't have the faintest idea how hard this is for me, do you?"

"Well, you purposely kept me out of the loop. What do you want?"

"Yeah, well, maybe even I believed you'd be able to make everything better. Waltz in with your big goofy smile and suck this thing out of me. But it's getting worse. And Dr. Singer is helping me realize what I'm capable of. I've lived with it for three years, each year watching it get progressively worse. And this is all I can give right now. I'm stuck—which means you're stuck. And you deserve more."

Have no idea what to say. Just continue to stir the melted ice cream, flabbergasted. Feel that she's making no sense *and* all the sense in the world. Feel yourself being boxed into a corner. Begin to get pissed off. Prepare to lash out.

When she says, "I guess it's like Woody Allen said, 'A relationship is like a shark—it has to keep moving forward or else it dies—'" cut her off before she finishes the quote. You know Woody Allen better than she does. You could quote the next five lines from that film if you wanted to.

Lash out: "What the *fuck* are you talking about?"

This will catch her off guard because you've never sworn at

her before. Her nose will twitch. She'll look through you instead of at you.

"Don't you still love me?"

"Of course I do. That's why this is so hard. Don't you get it? Dr. Singer says—"

Really raising your voice now: "Who gives a shit what Dr. Singer says!"

"I do!" she'll scream, upping the ante. "Listen to me, would you?!"

At this moment, the two of you will look up to find Charlene, your friendly waitress, standing there, sorry to be intruding but nonetheless wondering if she can get you anything else because she has to close out the bill.

Sonja will say, "Yeah—a white flag."

———•———

Back at the train station, stand by her side in complete silence. It will be foggy out, just like that first night on the beach, only the mood couldn't be more disparate now. Notice that no one else on the platform is speaking either. Like one of those E.F. Hutton commercials, only not really.

There will be nothing to say. By now she's repeated herself a hundred times: "You're worthy of so much more," "someone who can give you children," "a normal relationship," blabidy-fucking-blah. She'll sound like a mind-numbing looped Epcot announcement ("The path is moving at the same speed as the car. Please take small children by the hand. Please exit to your left . . .").

As you stand there feeling like your world is coming undone, do not lash out again. Maintaining good form is important when being dumped—especially in a dense fog. You don't need her remembering you as a selfish, heavy-handed loudmouth. Try to keep it together. Try to shine in your failure. Like that time back in the

PAL basketball league when you took a breakaway in the wrong direction. In your excitement, you mistook all the people screaming *"No! No!"* for *"Go! Go!"* Yet your father still says he never saw anyone display such good form in making a layup—and that's more important than scoring for the wrong team.

When the train comes, kiss her one last time, and then again on the forehead, but say nothing.

Tears will be winding down her cheeks as she says, "Be good."

Step onto the train—it will smell like burnt rubber. Stand by the doors and let them close in front of you. Wave. Let the train pull away. No, not yet. Wait. Wait. Not yet. Wait. Okay—now you can lose it.

II

THE NEXT MORNING, call in sick to work and spend the entire day buried under a winter-weight comforter. Get up only to urinate, defecate, or vomit.

III

THE NEXT DAY will be Saturday. Spend the greater part of this day in bed as well, getting up only to let Hal in, who's brought deli meats and a pecan pie. He'll spread everything out on your kitchen table and force you to sit with him.

He'll make a miniature turkey sandwich for you and move it slowly through the air to your lips while humming the theme song to *Jaws.*

Turn your head like a belligerent child. You're anything but hungry. In fact, the smell of the meat is starting to make you nauseous again.

Forever the actuary, he'll say, "Come on, man, you have to eat something. How about a nice piece of pecan 3.14?"

Run to the bathroom again. Hear Hal's voice trailing after you, "Oh, come on. The pun wasn't that bad, was it?"

IV

ON MONDAY, drag your sorry ass to work. Be happy for the distraction. Apply yourself (for a change) to the new PowerPoint presentation your boss has asked you to create for his upcoming trip to London.

Alexis will notice that you've lost a little weight. She'll say that it's especially important to eat when you're sick to replenish important nutrients lost along the way. Then she'll offer you a chocolate Krispy Kreme and a bag of Skittles.

V

SPEND ALL YOUR TIME outside the office watching who knows what on TV. Infomercials, *Sanford and Son* reruns, curling competitions—it will all be a blur. Don't go to the gym, don't return your parents' concerned phone calls, and don't open your mail. Look in the mirror from time to time and notice hairs appearing from your ears. Don't pluck them. Just notice them. This is what your life has come to: You are no longer a doer; you are an observer. You are no longer a participant—in fact, you aren't even the audience. You're canned laughter, minus the laughter. Go back to the mirror. Wonder how you're going to right the ship.

VI

ONE DAY AFTER WORK, fumbling through midtown, almost get hit by an MTA bus as you cross the street in a daze. This will shake you. For six whole hours you'll snap out of your depression. You'll sing "Zip-a-Dee-Doo-Dah" as you prepare a cheese omelet for dinner. (Be sure to put in extra onions.)

However, when you wake the next morning and see Sonja's photograph on your fridge, slip right back to your cameo role in *Day of the Living Dead.*

VII

THE NEXT WEEK, cancel your therapy session. Come to the conclusion that you need a break from it until you've had time to sort through your feelings.

Call Sonja when you know she'll be in class just to hear her voice on the voice mail. Do this two more times over the next few days. Tear up a little each time you hang up before the beep.

VIII

THE FOLLOWING WEEK, receive a call at the office from a perky-sounding young woman.

"This is Simon, Gill, and Silverstein," she'll squeak. "I have Mr. Silverstein on the phone for you."

Shoot upright in your chair. Listen carefully as the familiar voice comes booming across your speakerphone.

"So I finally got around to reading the script!" He'll sound excited, like he's just been on the phone with Columbia Pictures, who are ready to offer a two-picture deal.

"Oh? Really?"

"There's a lot of good stuff in there."

Okay, now he sounds a little less enthusiastic. Maybe it's just a straightforward one-picture deal.

"I'm glad you liked it."

"Yeah. Tell me, the ending, is that set in stone?"

Why? Does Columbia have a better idea? "Oh, no! Absolutely not."

He'll say, "That's good, because it's kind of a disappointment. I mean, the world doesn't need another David Lynch—you know what I'm saying?"

Then he'll ask if you're married to New York City, because there's a new sitcom being developed by some producers he knows. They're looking for absurd comic writers—especially fresh faces who've never worked in Hollywood before.

Though the idea of living in a place where people get in their cars to drive to the neighbor's house scares the bejesus out of you, tell Silverstein there's really nothing keeping you in New York and you'd be thrilled to be a part of any show he thought was right for you.

"Great!" he'll say.

The show's called *When Martial Arts Jump the Shark* and is about two Asian American homosexual men named Marshall and Art who live in Eugene, Oregon.

Laugh at the thought of this. It will be the first time you've laughed in two weeks. Laugh several more times when he explains the premise of the show: Marshall and Art own their own martial arts studio, which, in addition to offering standard karate lessons, offers classes like kung nu-doo—a synergy of kung fu and a complete hair makeover.

Silverstein will go on to explain how the producers are hoping to beat the critics to the punch by adding "Jump the Shark" to the show's title.

You grew up with *Happy Days*. You know all about the famous shark-jump episode—though personally you think the show jumped a lot earlier. Like when Potsie started singing on a regular basis.

Silverstein will say, "So we'd need you out here next month. Does that give you enough time?"

Tell him it's probably fine. That you'll need to take care of some things, like finding a sublet for your current lease and buying a car, but once you get your ducks in a row, it'll be doable.

IX

SPEND THE NEXT FEW DAYS leaving messages on Sonja's voice mail—she'll be the first person you'll want to hear the news. When she doesn't return your calls, send her the following brief e-mail:

It looks like I might be moving to LA. Got a writing gig. Can we talk?

Later that day, receive her response:

I always believed in you. See, all it took was someone like Silverstein to believe in you. As for talking, I'm not sure it's a good idea. While this is no picnic for me either, I think conversation would only complicate things. The last thing you need now is something tying you down here. Go West, young man. Go West! There's gold in dem der hills. Once the smog clears, I'm fairly certain you'll find it.

HOW TO COMPLETE A TO-DO LIST

I

1) ~~Sublet apt.~~

2) ~~Freak out (!)~~

3) ~~Get a grip . . .~~

4) ~~Deal with spare keys~~

5) ~~Cancel gym membership~~

6) Dad's b-day

Board an Amtrak train headed for Philadelphia. You'll be visiting your parents on the occasion of your father's sixty-first birthday. Be sure to bring along that new SpiderWire fishing line you bought for him. Remember how you asked the cashier, Wanda, at the sporting goods store to wrap it for you. And she looked at you as if you should be able to wrap a little spool of fishing line yourself. Back at home, you struggled for fifteen minutes trying to wrap the damn thing, only to discover that electrical tape doesn't hold shiny wrapping paper together the way it does charred toaster oven plugs. Someone should write a book for the single guy: a simple instructional book with lavish color photos illustrating the dos and don'ts of present wrapping.

———•———

A young, overly affectionate couple in the seat across the way will spend entirely too much time cuddling and cooing.

"You're beautiful."

"No, you're beautiful."

"No, *you're* beautiful."

"No, YOU'RE beautiful."

With more force than necessary, yank your ticket out of that thingamabob on top of the seat and seek out another spot.

———•———

In your new seat, stare lazily out the window as the train passes Trenton, New Jersey. A huge electric sign spanning the length of the bridge over the Delaware River that normally reads

    TRENTON MAKES—THE WORLD TAKES

will read:

    TRENTON MAKES—THE WORLD AKE .

I guess they don't call New Jersey "the armpit of the nation" for nothing.

———•———

Time with your parents will pass like kidney stones—slowly and with great difficulty. There's nothing worse than a mother doting on a recently dumped son, especially when she liked his girlfriend.

The breakup was rough enough. The last thing you need is your mother pouring reconstituted lemon juice into the wound.

"Well, did you try to change her mind? Talk some reason into her?"

"Yes, Mom, I tried to change her mind."

"Were you persistent? Sometimes a girl just needs a little convincing."

"Yes, Mom, I was persistent."

"I just don't understand—she was such a lovely young woman."

"Yes, Mom, she was such lovely young woman."

———•———

Your family will have the strange tradition of giving presents on birthdays in addition to receiving them. When you were a kid, giveaways included lollipops and packs of gum. In more recent years, on your parents' birthdays, they've given you things like furniture for your apartment or coupons redeemable for courtside Sixers tickets.

This year, with your father going into early retirement and you going out West, don't be surprised when he comes forward with a nice fat check.

"This," he'll say with silly dramatic bravado, "is to help with that car you'll need out in Hollywood."

At first you'll think it says $1,000, but when you look more closely and count the zeros, you'll see that it actually reads $10,000.

Open your eyes as wide as they'll go and let out a deep-bellied, "Whoa."

He'll grab your face and kiss you on both cheeks like you're suddenly an Italian or Greek family from the old country.

From your mother you'll get a slightly less spirited kiss and a lot of grief along these lines:

"Well, I just don't like the idea of you driving cross-country by yourself. Remember what happened to your cousin Louis? Now paraplegic, if you've forgotten."

Cousin Louis was walking to his car in a mall parking lot five miles from his house when a drunken motorcyclist struck him, but this is the same thing as driving cross-country as far as your mother is concerned.

II

7) ~~Cancel magazines~~

8) ~~Call DMV, get them to send form to renew license~~

9) ~~Call DMV, get them to send correct form to renew license~~

10) Quit work

You've been fantasizing about this day ever since you signed your contract two years ago. A hefty advance for your first script would arrive and be promptly deposited in your bank account, and the very next day you'd march straight into your boss's office and say, "Excuse me, but may I have a word with you?" Your boss would motion for you to shut his office door and sit down. With the strong sun bouncing off the Hudson River creating an intense glare behind him, you'd narrow your eyes into a tight squint and scream, "PARTY TIME'S OVER, BABY! I SOLD A SCRIPT! I SOLD A SCRIPT! WHOOOO HOOOOO!!! I SOLD A SCRIPT!" Then you'd dance your chicken dance around his office—whipping him into a red-faced frenzy before heading off to pack your belongings.

"YOU'RE FIRED!" he'd scream after you—storming out to grab a couple security guards just in case you're packing a revolver.

Fired? you'd think to yourself. *Didn't I just quit?*

But as it turns out, there's no hefty advance for sitcom work— the trip out to LA will be made off your flimsy savings account— and if you want money for gas and tolls, you're going to have to comply with the firm's rigid two-weeks' notification policy to collect that last paycheck. Talk about throwing cold water on YOU'RE FIRED.

———◆———

As usual, Alexis will be the first to poke her nose into your business. "So I hear ya quittin'," she'll say, scratching at her head with a ballpoint pen.

Seeing as you haven't told your boss yet, or anyone else in the office, wonder how Alexis could possibly know this. Has she been reading your e-mails over your shoulder? Has she been eavesdropping on your private phone conversations?

"Really? Who told you that?"

"Oh, come awn," she'll say with a coy smile. "If ya haven't figured it auwt yet, I know all the dirt 'round he-er."

Wish that you could call Sonja like you used to and tell her how Alexis just pronounced the word *here* with two syllables. In fact, wish that you could still tell Sonja half the stuff that comes out of her mouth, not to mention her friends'. Last week, for instance, a gay friend of hers named Chuck with blown-out dyed blond hair (and eyebrows), who works in Facilities on the second floor, came up to her cubicle and called out, "Alexis, *honey,* I've been waiting downstairs for ten minutes! Lift and separate—let's GOOO!"

———◆———

Sit with your boss and quietly give your two weeks' notice. Spot a tiny picture frame sitting under his computer monitor. As he thanks you for your hard work and dedication to the team, let the photograph in the frame steal your attention. It'll be a picture of him and his wife holding two babies in their arms. Given that your boss has probably looked exactly the same in every photograph since the eighth grade, it will be hard to tell if it's a recent photo—but as far as you know, he doesn't have any children.

After he rises to shake your hand, very cautiously inquire about the photo. Ask him whose children they are.

"Ohh!" he'll say, more animated than usual. "Didn't I tell you? My wife and I had twins! Yeah. A few weeks ago. It's amazing. We were trying to get pregnant for an entire year, but nothing, nothing, nothing. Then, one day, boom! Twins! I don't know—I guess all good things come to those who wait. Right?"

Congratulate him as you leave his office. Though you'll think it just a bit off that he didn't share this news with anyone on your team, allow yourself to feel a touch envious knowing that he's a father—and one several years younger than you at that.

Go over to your desk and sit down. Look at the calendar. Nine days until the big three-oh. Try to look on the bright side (there's always a bright side): At least you won't be working as an admin. asst. this time next year.

Alexis will call over from her cubicle: "So? Ya give two weeks yet or wat?"

Another bright side (can there be two bright sides?): no Alexis! Without sounding like a smart aleck, say, "I'm sorry, I don't really see how that's any of your business, Alexis."

With a big shrug, she'll say, "Wateva-wateva."

III

11) ~~Get mail forwarding form from PO~~

12) ~~Get correct mail forwarding form from PO~~

13) Final shrink session

This will be the first time you're seeing your therapist in about a month. The last time you were here you stormed out in a huff—something you're more than mildly ashamed of now.

By way of apology and as an appropriate farewell gift, bring her a good-size flowering orchid plant. According to Hal's wife, Erin, women adore them. And here you always thought chrysanthemums at $8.95/dozen said, "I'm sorry." Boy, were you off the mark—like seventy-five dollars off the mark.

Placing the orchid on the windowsill, she'll say, "You really don't need to apologize. It's quite all right."

"Well, it's also my way of thanking you for all you've done over the last couple of years."

"You should be thanking yourself," she'll say quite seriously. "You did all the work. All I did was listen and make a suggestion every now and again."

"And for that I paid you one hundred dollars an hour?! Give me that orchid—I'm taking it back."

She'll guffaw.

"I'm serious. Hand it over."

———•———

Take your time recapping the breakup. Hearing the story out loud will help you gain some objectivity. No, it won't—who are you kidding?

When you've finished, your therapist will clear her throat and say, "How did you feel just now, telling me all that?"

Think about her question for at least a minute, perhaps more. Like a silent hiccup, the word *lint* will keep recurring in your mind.

Say: "You know that feeling when you clean the lint out of the dryer tray?"

"I think so. Why?"

"That's what it felt like. I don't know about you, but when I take my hand and scrape out the lint tray, it kind of makes me feel good, especially when it all comes off in one piece—like a great big patch of lint, if that makes any sense."

"Are you saying that talking about your breakup makes you feel like a big patch of lint?"

To the very end, you can always count on her for a good laugh.

"What I think I'm saying is I may have to carry this big piece of dirt around for a while, but in the meantime, I'm happy to have gotten it out of the tray."

"Well, you should be warned," she'll say, chuckling through her words. "People spend their entire lives just trying to find a trash can."

———•———

When your time is up, she'll wish you luck out on the coast and offer phone sessions should you not find someone you click with out there. Thank her again and then, bashfully, ask if you can give her a hug. She'll be embarrassed by this, as if you just asked her to break official Psychoanalysts' Code of Conduct Rule #407 (Never let your clothing come in contact with the patient's—especially if he or she owns a cat), but will nonetheless wrap her arms heartily around you and express her wish that you keep in touch.

———•———

Spend the next couple of hours in her elevator thinking about how much you'll miss her affable, welcoming smile. Wonder who's going to take her place once you get out there—or if, indeed, you'll prefer phone sessions. Begin to calculate the cost of a weekly forty-five-minute call from LA to NYC during off-peak hours: *52 times 45 times .1, let's see, right, and carry the one, and, hmmm . . .*

IV

14) ~~Get a physical before insurance runs out~~

15) ~~Go to the dentist before insurance runs out~~

16) ~~Get new orthodics before insurance runs out~~

17) ~~Get new insurance before insurance runs out~~

18) Buy car

For a guy your age who's into sports, curiously, you know very little about cars. Especially the goings-on under the hood. In fact, if it weren't for the few riotous episodes of Click and Clack's *Car Talk* you've listened to recently, you would have already purchased the inexpensive Yugo—a car, it turns out, that doesn't let yu-go anywhere except the auto repair shop.

As far as you're concerned, a "transmission" is the dialogue between NASA control and an astronaut on the moon. "Alternators" are annoying people who can't seem to stick to one lane on the expressway. A "condensor" is someone who knows how to make his point in as few words as possible. For example, in your freshman year of college there was a guy across the quad named Alfie who'd condense "John, do you want to go get some pizza now?" (eleven syllables) into the following two syllables: "Dude, za?"

A "starter" is the guy who fires the gun at track and field competitions. An "auxiliary fan" is Hal's wife, Erin, who spends all her time at the ball game commenting on which cold beer peddlers are cute and which players need baggier uniforms. A "shock" is something you get when you catch your parents having sex. A "belt" holds your pants up. The "clutch" is something one comes through in, and an "intake manifold" is, well, anyone's guess.

———•———

Go to the Volkswagen showroom on Eleventh Avenue. You'll be meeting with Dwayne, who you've talked to several times on the phone. When you get there, he'll ask you to sit in a small room that smells like wet socks and to fill out a questionnaire to help him understand exactly what kind of car you're looking for. Then he'll ask if you'd like a cup of coffee. Break your rule about not letting complete strangers fix coffee for you—especially ones wearing baseball caps that say "Jesus Is My Homeboy"—and set about answering the questions.

Q: How many miles per year do you think you will put on this vehicle?

A: *Too many—I'll be making frequent cross-country trips.*

Q: On average, how many hours per day will you be spending in the car?

A: *Too many—I'll be stuck in bumper-to-bumper traffic raza-fraza-ing up a small storm.*

Q: What type of driving will you be doing in this vehicle?

A: *Good driving?*

Q: What can you comfortably put down now?

A: *This pen.*

Dwayne will come back with coffee and take you into the showroom.

Looking over the questionnaire, he'll chuckle and say, "Well, judging from some of your answers, you'd be better off buying a mobile home."

"You know, that's actually not a bad idea. What do they go for?"

———•———

Test-drive the Jetta and the Passat. When you're done, tell Dwayne that you couldn't tell any difference between the two.

"Really? Well, while they both have an I-4 cylinder configuration and a 1.8-liter engine, the Passat blows the Jetta away with its one hundred ninety horsepower. It's also got one hundred sixty-six feet torque, twenty valves compared to the Jetta's eight, and a compression ratio of nine-to-one, which should . . ."

Apparently he thinks you know cars. Meanwhile you're not getting a word of what he's saying. Like the way you don't get why models—the prettiest women in the world—always look so angry. ("Goddamn it, I *hate* being this hot. I can't stand all these gorgeous clothes. Life rots.")

When he's done, say, "Riiiiiight. Tell me, Dwayne, which one has a better sound system?"

"Oh, they both come equipped with our standard antitheft components and eight Monsoon speakers."

Tilt your head to one side like you're weighing the options. Take one last walk around both cars. Run your finger over the hood of the Jetta. Kick the tires.

Say: "I'll take whichever one is cheaper"—a decision you could have made by phone, but hey, you'd have missed out on a free cup of the muddiest coffee of your life.

v

19) ~~Go to Radio Shack and buy radar detector for cross-country trip~~

20) ~~Be sure to put radar detector receipt in a safe place so that you can return the thing at another Radio Shack once you've arrived in LA~~

21) Turn thirty.

Wake up in the morning and go straight to the mirror. Pull at your skin. Inspect your nostrils. Note new wrinkles under your eyes and more black hairs shooting wildly from not only the tips of your ears but now from the earlobes as well. Wonderful.

It will be Sunday. Spend the entire morning waiting for Sonja to call. If there were ever an excuse for her to get back in touch, this would be it. When you go down for the paper, take both the cell and the cordless phone with you. Every time one of them rings, feel your stomach pop a wheelie around your liver. Be happy that your old college roommate Jeff's calling, that your cousin Susan's calling, but ever so slightly crestfallen that they're not Sonja.

See no one all morning but the Korean deli owner, Doo-Hwan. For years you've been trying to explain the humor in his name—changing the lyrics of "Da Doo Ron Ron" to "the doo-hwan hwan, the doo-hwan hwan"—but to no avail. When you see him, tell him it's your thirtieth birthday in an attempt to get a free box of Chiclets out of such a distinguished day.

He'll say, "Ohhh! Thirty! Really? Ahhh. Nice. I remember thirty. Was terrible year. Fucking shit year. Wife died. Nearly lost mind. Nearly lost business. What fucking shit year. But hey! Good for you! Thirty. Nice. Ahhh. Sixty cents for Chiclets."

———•———

When you get home from the deli, the red light on your answering machine will be blinking. Apparently the cordless's range didn't reach to the corner. Wring your hands. Throw an oar. Press "play" on the machine and feel your heart kick it up a notch.

The female machine voice—the only woman who's lasted more than a year in your apartment—will say: "Eeww ave (pause) WON mmmesege."

The tape will rewind with a lot of clunking and get ready to play.

"Hi, it's Mom. Whelp, I believe someone's celebrating his thirtieth birthday today! God! I can't believe I have a son thirty years old! Dad's out at the market; he'll call you later. Is the weather as crappy up there as it is here? Oh, and did you get that stuff I sent in the mail? How come you never respond? A simple thank-you would suffice. A simple, 'Yes, Mom, I got the stuff you sent in the mail.' Is that too hard for you to . . ."

Be relieved that you didn't miss a call from Sonja but slightly frustrated that you've got to sit there for ten minutes as your mother goes on and on and on. She'll take up half the tape with her message—and not just because it's your birthday. This is a weekly occurrence. And probably true of many if not all mothers across the tri-state area. They won't just say, "Call me back—I've got some things to discuss." Every last thing they want to tell or ask must be left on the machine before they're capable of returning receiver to cradle. Of course the irony is that when they're six feet under, it's the thing you'll miss most—the weekly monologue on the machine. Tapes you'd wished you'd saved.

———•———

Continue to cross things off and add new items to your to-do list:

22) ~~Pack supplies: two-inch brass fasteners, three-hole punch, etc.~~

23) ~~Take posters off bathroom wall~~

24) Pack Sonja's clothes and toothbrush

Just after dinner, the phone will ring again. By this time you've started to give up hope that she'll call, which is a good thing because Hal's voice will be on the other end.

"Hey."

"Yo."

"Fuckin' A. Huh?"

"Tell me about it."

Hal will run down the list of guests he's invited to a party he and Erin are throwing for you up in Rye, where they've recently moved.

Say: "Why are you inviting Ted Barkowski?" an old friend who has drifted.

"What's wrong with Ted?"

"I don't know. Nothing, I guess. It's just that the guy insists on telling that stupid weak back joke at every party. 'Oh, Doctor, I've got a weak back. When did you get it? About a week back.' Ha-ha, Ted, that's hilarious."

"Listen to you. Are you hearing the same jaded, bitter crap that I'm hearing?"

"Oh, come on, give me a break."

"Seriously. I'm telling you. You're inches away from curmudgeonhood—and you've only turned thirty today. I can only imagine what you're going to sound like when you're forty."

"Yeah. Well. Talk to me in a month when you're turning thirty and we'll see just how well you're handling it."

But the truth is, this isn't about turning thirty at all, and you know it. This is about Sonja. And nothing—not a party up in Rye, not a $10,000 check, not even a writing job out in LA—can take away the assiduous dull thrum of an ache that makes you feel like vomiting each and every morning when you wake up. Though perhaps there's one thing that can provide some temporary relief. And that's a call-waiting beep with a 516 number on your caller ID.

———————•———————

"Hi."

"Hi."

If you thought your heart was pounding before, now it will be leaping through your chest cavity.

"How are you?"

"You know. I'm . . . well . . . I'm thirty." Chuckle. "That pretty much sums it up."

As she asks how you've spent the day, feel an overwhelming desire to tell her how you waited by the phone for this very moment. You'll want to scream out how much you still love her—how you miss her more, not less, with each day. But don't. Don't say what's on your mind. Bad timing. Maybe the opportunity will arise later. Be patient. For now, just tell her you've been busy packing, organizing, taking birthday calls, saying good-bye to Doo-Hwan.

"No party?" she'll ask.

"Next weekend. Hal and Erin are throwing a combination going-away slash belated birthday party."

"Oh. That's nice."

"Yeah. I'll go up there with all my things packed in—ohh, yeah, I didn't tell you: I bought a car."

"Really?"

"Yeah. Can you believe it? Me? The guy who refuses to drive the golf course?"

"What kind?"

"Jetta. White. Well, off-white, really."

"That fits you."

"You think?"

"Mm-hmm."

Have a split-second fantasy in which the two of you are driving around the Hamptons in your new car. Her sitting shotgun with her stockinged feet up on the dashboard, like you used to see your mother do.

"Yeah, so I'll drive it up to Hal's with all my stuff, have the party, spend the night, and then get up early Sunday morning and, well . . . 'go west,' as you said."

"Exciting."

"Yeah. Kind of."

Ask her how she is.

"Fine. Studying hard."

Ask her how Jess and Merrill are. She'll say well. Jess hosted a synagogue sisterhood fund-raising auction and Merrill wound up high bidder on a six-month cruise around the world.

"Can you believe it?"

"Wow."

"Yeah. They're so excited. They leave tomorrow morning."

Ask her if Merrill's bringing his power drill for rainy day activities on the Lido deck. She'll emit that little giggle that slips out through her teeth—the one that helped you fall in love with her all those months ago. For a moment, it will feel like old times, like nothing ever changed. But then, with a flicker, the moment will pass, leaving an awkward silence in its wake.

Fill the space with small talk—something about the show you'll be working on and how your sports teams are doing. Nagging at you in the back of your mind will be the question: Don't you miss me?

For a fleeting second, consider asking if she's back on the Internet dating site but don't you dare. Anyway, you know she's not—you've checked every day for the last several weeks.

The conversation will feel like it's running out of steam. Like at any moment one of you will say, "Well . . ." the universal signal for "Let's wrap this thing up." In the old days you never had to think of things to say with Sonja. Ten, sometimes fifteen, mini-conversations would be open at any given time. Tangents, digressions, non sequiturs—all flowing naturally from one to the next: a dialogue jigsaw puzzle connected by curvy corners and bowl-shaped inlets.

And the thing that bothers you so much now is this: In essence, nothing's changed. A month has passed, that's all. You know she still loves you. You know she misses you. You know it could all be restored if one of you had the guts to explore the realm of possibilities rather than simply joking with the Friendly's waitress about a fucking white flag.

"Well, I guess I'll let you go," Sonja will say, tears lurking behind her words.

"Okay. It was nice of you to call. I was kind of wondering if you would."

"Yeah."

Silence.

More silence.

"Oh, you didn't say anything about the script. Is Silverstein going to try to sell it for you?"

"Not now. He didn't like the ending. Said I need to rewrite the last act. Something slightly, I don't know, more realistic."

"And how do you feel about that?"

"I guess. Maybe. To tell you the truth, I've been so busy getting ready for this move, I haven't really thought about it much. Endings are hard. You know? They're the hardest parts to get right."

"Right."

So much silence you think your ears are going to explode. And then, finally:

"Well, you be good," and the sound of Sonja burying the phone into a pillow or something.

Wait for her to add something. When she doesn't, say, "Yeah. Okay. You too. Thanks again for calling . . . snowflake."

———•———

Wait several hours for a callback that will never come. Slump into bed. Toss and turn for at least an hour. Turn on the light and fumble for your to-do list. Add one last thing—to be finished in the morning:

25) Ship Sonja's clothes, toothbrush, etc. to Baldwin

Welcome to your thirties.

HOW TO FINISH A SCREENPLAY

I

HAL AND ERIN'S NEW PLACE in Rye will be set back in a wooded area off a quiet tree-lined street. The sky above it will be sandpaper gray. A light freezing rain will begin to fall just as you arrive. They had been promising the winter's first snow on the radio, but so far, just the rain. The driveway will be full of cars, forcing you to park on the street—a maneuver made exceptionally difficult by your life's belongings piled high on the backseat. A sliver of rearview will be all that's left.

Accidentally bump into the car behind you, setting off a curious speaking car alarm: "Perimeter violation! Perimeter violation! Alarm in five, four, three, two . . ." Followed by a rousing chorus of trills, sirens, honks, and flashing lights.

Welcome to the suburbs. Take away the freezing rain, exchange the maple trees for palms, and this will be your life three thousand miles from now. Fabulous.

———•———

Walk up an old cobblestone path to the front door and ring the bell. As you wait, suddenly imagine Sonja and Hal on the phone some days earlier, secretly plotting a surprise. Your heart will kick into overdrive. Ring again. When Erin appears in the doorway, rush in, expecting to see Sonja atop the stairwell. Not there. Okay, maybe back there, behind the Christmas tree. No. Over there? Next to the piano?

"Everything okay?" Erin will ask.

"Sonja's not here, is she?"

"Did you want us to invite her?" Erin will say with an apologetic look on her face. "We just assumed that . . ."

"No. Christ, no. That would've been a little awkward, right? If she had been invited?"

"Right."

———•———

People will already be on their second round of drinks when you come into the living room. Greet everyone with an apology: Your sublet took the wrong subway and wound up in Queens. When she finally got to your place, she'd forgotten the keys you'd mailed to her and an extra set had to be made before you could get on the road. This will all be an extravagant fabrication, of course. The truth being that you were once again struck down with nasty flatulence and had to wait an hour for the GastroSoothe to kick in so as not to desecrate that uniquely wonderful new car smell.

A double-layer chocolate cake will be brought out with white icing that says:

Hollywood in the 30s – What Could Be Better?
Mazzel Tov!

Don't bother telling Erin, who probably stayed up late last night baking the thing, that *mazel* only has one Z. Besides, who are you to correct anyone? As Hal likes to point out, you still incorrectly refer to the sixteenth century as "the Reconnaissance."

Look around the room as everyone sings "Happy Birthday." Wonder who half these people are. Friends of Hal's? Erin's? People they needed to invite to pad the party? To make it look like a real party? In their old Manhattan apartment, there'd be no need. The fewer people the better. Now, in the suburbs, in a living room you could land the Goodyear blimp in, party padders with plastic kazoos have been brought in to help create the proper festive atmosphere.

Blow out the candles. Clap. Wonder where your twenties went.

———•———

Observe Ted Barkowski near the fireplace telling two unsuspecting padders his weak back joke. When he gets to the punch line, watch them stare blankly, wondering if there's more to it.

"You get it?" Ted will say with a screwed-up smile on his face. "A *week* back?"

Ted will notice you looking on. Go immediately from the room and get in line for some hot grog.

———•———

Some old friends from your ad agency days will wonder if you've already lined up an apartment. Tell them that your agent is letting you stay in his guest room until you find your own place. Get a rise out of saying "my agent." Say it a few more times during the conversation. Wonder if this is what it feels like to say, "my wife."

Over the last couple of years you've become jealous of people who say things like: "My wife is out of town" or "My wife and I liked that film." These are obviously men who've recently married.

After about three years of marriage, "my wife," morphs into "we," as in "We accidentally drank the water in Mexico last year," or, after forty years of marriage, "We don't like the thermostat set above sixty-eight."

———•———

When everyone's gone, sit around the fireplace with Hal and Erin and their golden retriever, Munch. It'll be a good thing you're buzzed from all the grog, otherwise the idea of sitting with a big old dog in front of a big old roaring fire in a big old comfy house would be torturous. You'd be suffocated by envy.

Erin, a second-grade teacher, who, at the age of thirty-two, has somehow managed to hold on to her childhood dimples, will say, "So we have some good news," with a glowing smile that can mean only one thing.

Your jaw on the floor, say, "Nooo! Are you kidding me?! And you're only telling me now?! I don't believe this!"

Hal will say, "We wanted to wait until we had you to our-selves."

Okay, so now you're dealing with the roaring fire, the big old comfy house, a golden retriever who refuses to release your arm from its jaws, *and* an expecting couple. At this point you might want to consider spending the night in a nearby Motel 6.

"Holy cow. That's amazing! I'm shocked."

"So were we," Erin will say, reaching for Hal's hand like they're suddenly being interviewed on *E! True Hollywood Story.*

"Yeah," Hal will say, "it wasn't planned at all—but hey, you know that joke about making God laugh, right?"

With a touch of grief in your voice, say, "Know it? I think I wrote it."

———•———

A couple of hours later, Erin will show you where you're sleeping and hand you fresh towels that reek of fabric softener. This will be interesting because you've often noticed how dryers in the city tend to suck all the fabric softener out of your clothes. Sure, the clothes are plenty soft, but what about that fresh windblown scent? Even if you put two softener sheets in the dryer, still nothing. And now you have your answer. Apparently there's a direct pipeline out the back of every coin-op laundry in Manhattan that feeds into the laundry rooms of millions of homes from Rye to Scarsdale, from Dobbs Ferry to Hastings. And no one knows about this except you. Thieves!

Wonder if the situation is the same all across the country. With Chicago feeding Evanston—Boston, Newton. Consider mentioning your discovery to Erin, but wisely refrain. Take the towels from her and thank her again for the party. Tell her it was the best birthday slash going-away party you've ever had. And you mean that.

Hal will come in just as Erin is leaving. He'll sit down on the bed with you and ask if you've got everything you need.

With a sardonic, tight smile say, "Are you speaking metaphorically?"

He'll lean back against the cast-iron headboard and say that's exactly what he came in to talk to you about.

"What, metaphors?"

"Sure, metaphors. Why not? This is the perfect place for them. All those birches out there—the high stone wall running behind that little creek in the backyard."

"And that's just the Robert Frost-ing on the cake, which, by the way, was fantastic. Erin bake it herself?"

"I mixed the batter, if that counts as helping."

"Nice. You guys make a good pair."

He'll try to pun off *pair*—something about a pear tart—but

won't carry it off well. Blaming the "half-baked" attempt on his semi-inebriated state.

As he gets his conversational bearings back—blabbering on about regrets he's tallied up over the years—let a feeling of content come over you. Content to be spending your last night in New York with Hal. In his big house with the quiet central heating blowing through the little brown vent by your leg. The same Hal who, at the age of fourteen, would unfailingly blame his loss to you at Atari Football on a busted joystick. The same Hal who'd drive eight hours to Penn State just to spend a weekend hanging out when his finals were over before yours. The same Hal who talked you into taking that screenwriting course with Joseph Stalin and who is right now helping you make sense of your relationship with Sonja—just to make sure you don't feel like it was all for nothing or regret what might have been.

"Everybody has that one person," he'll say as he shifts his weight from one side to the other. "That one person they think about every day but don't speak to for one reason or another. That one person who helped make them who they are—even if they're not aware of it yet." He'll pause for a second and pull at his earlobe a few times—like he's suddenly a third-base coach giving hit-and-run signs. "Maybe Sonja was that person for you. The someone who gets you ready for the right someone who comes along next. Or soon after next. Maybe she upped the ante—helped you confront the possibility of growing up, of commitment—so next time, you'll be ready."

Say nothing in response. Just nod your head to let him know you appreciate what he's said—and that you're trying to see things from his perspective. Trying to move on with your life without regret—metaphoric or otherwise. Of all the people you'll miss this time tomorrow, while settling into a cheap motel with a strip of paper across the toilet seat that reads SANITIZED FOR YOUR PRO-

TECTION, Hal tops the list easily. Well, Sonja, then Hal, but that goes without saying.

II

IN THE MORNING, over black coffee and bagels, sit with Hal and Erin and review the directions your father sent you off the Internet. Discovering MapQuest.com has given your father a renewed interest in life. Even more technologically inept than you, he can't manage to download a simple photo attachment from his e-mail, but boy can he MapQuest. Doesn't matter if it's a little jaunt to the market, a five-mile trip to the art museum, or a three-hour ride to a relative's house—he must MapQuest them. And it doesn't stop with the immediate family. If he's at a party and overhears a complete stranger talking about an upcoming trip, he'll MapQuest it—sometimes providing an alternate route from Yahoo! as well. Other than his boat, nothing gives the man more pleasure than printing out driving directions. And after three years of doing it, he shows no signs of diminished enthusiasm. Every single time he hits print, he can be heard off in the study, singing the website's praises: "Amazing! Simply amazing! I don't know how they do it!"

"I don't care what MapQuest says," Hal will remark. "It doesn't know what kind of construction is happening on 287. I'm telling you: Take I-95 to the George Washington Bridge. You'll save yourself thirty minutes at least."

———•———

Getting on the road will take more time that you'd planned. Separation anxiety and a general feeling of panic will suddenly overwhelm you, necessitating several trips to the bathroom to relieve bloating and the runs.

Finally, after a protracted send-off with lots of hugs—Erin

running back to the house at the last minute for sandwiches—and more hugs, you'll find yourself headed south on I-95 with the sky once again threatening snow.

Turn on the radio. Hit the scan button every few seconds. Sure, "Wheel in the Sky" is a good song, but "Sympathy for the Devil," or any Stones song for that matter, would be better.

Scan. Elvis. Scan. Generic rap. Scan. Heart—"Barracuda." Scan. Phil Collins! *SCAN!* "More Than a Woman." Not bad, but still—scan. Meanwhile, you've missed "Wheel in the Sky" entirely—the best song you've heard so far. Realize that this is the story of your life.

Realize that if you are to make a clean break from the past— from the East Coast—you're going to have to start now. Pick one fucking station and leave it on. That's it; leave it on until you lose reception. Until it melds into an evangelist program, into light classics or, worse, show tunes played on steel drums.

Leave it on, even though "House of the Rising Sun" brings back bad memories from your high school prom. Leave it on— past the exits for Harrison and Mamaroneck—even though the organ in "A Whiter Shade of Pale" makes you think of funeral parlors and open caskets.

As you pass through Mount Vernon, your number one all-time *least* favorite song in the world, "Bohemian Rhapsody" by Queen, will come on. At the very first sound of that annoying a cappella intro, you'll want to reach for the dial. But no! Don't do it! You mustn't! This is the new you. The mature, soon-to-be-successful West Coast version of you. If you must, turn off the radio. Just don't you dare change that dial.

Wish that you could go back to the VW showroom and do it all over again. Back to Dwayne with his purple "Jesus Is My Homeboy" baseball hat and splurge—yes, splurge, goddamn it—

on the optional CD player as "Galileo, Galileo" booms over and over again out of the Jetta's eight Monsoon speakers.

———•———

As you enter the Bronx and the first snowflake of winter lands on your windshield, there will be a sign warning you that the highway will soon divide. You'll have to get into the right lane to continue on 95 over the George Washington Bridge and into New Jersey. Veering left will take you to 295, over the Throgs Neck Bridge and into Long Island. The big, bold, white letters spelling out "Long Island" will cause you to forget all about Galileo and his Figaro magnifico. Ghosted images of parking lots and Midas mufflers will flash through your mind.

It will begin to snow harder. Your windshield wipers will grind loudly against the glass. Memories of Sonja will flutter to and fro, to and fro—in perfect rhythm.

swish

On the beach. You darting around the water's edge, imitating those funny little birds that scamper away from oncoming waves. Trying to get Sonja to do the same.

swish

In bed. Sonja curled around the façade of your body. Her bony knees sticking uncomfortably into the small of your back. The smell of makeup sex still hanging in the air. Dried makeup tears plastered against your cheeks.

swish

At Shea Stadium. Sonja rooting for the Mets while you root for your team, the Philadelphia Phillies. Sonja dumping a bag of peanuts on your head when Phillies first baseman, Jim Thome, hits a two-run home run in the top of the eighth.

And then, as if in suspended hypnosis, you and Sonja will become Drew and Marilyn. Actual memories will elide with scenes from your screenplay. You won't be able to tell what's real and what's fiction. Who had that fight on West Fourth Street, in front of the Belgian French fry place? Did you refer to Sonja as a snowflake, or was that something Drew called Marilyn? Who said "I love you" first? Who lives in Baldwin? Who went on the pill? Who quit his job?

And with another *swish* of the wipers, Joseph Stalin will be sitting with you, in the passenger seat. Only it won't be your teacher Joseph Stalin, it will be the *real* Joseph Stalin. And he'll be slamming his fist down on the glove compartment as he pontificates about third-act mechanics:

"Your protagonist *must* be nervous! He *must* be afraid! He *must* be insecure! Yes, *insecure*! You *must* write him in such a way that we feel his insecurities, his fear of the unknown. Just like we did when Hitler turned on us that frigid day back in '41. The audience *must* be rooting for the protagonist to conquer his fears. And to accomplish this efficiently, in less than thirty minutes, he *must* run toward the resolution. *Run!* Like a world-class sprinter runs to the finish line."

And as quickly as he appeared, with another *swish* Stalin will evaporate into the ether. Your heart will be soaring as you glance down at the speedometer and find that you're pushing 90 mph. Don't slow down. No, don't you dare slow down—even though the snow is beginning to stick to the road.

Begin to address someone out loud—someone sitting shotgun. Perhaps Hal. Perhaps your mother. It doesn't matter. Just so long as you think someone's listening.

"She's so unbelievably kind to me. You know? So unbelievably kind. She's the kindest person I ever met. And not just to me. To everyone! Isn't that more important than children?"

Give the Jetta some more gas. You'll be flying so fast now, the snow won't have a chance to settle on the windshield.

"Sure, she's got problems. So what? Who doesn't? Right? I've got problems. Jam Master Jay had 'em. Even Albert fucking Einstein had problems. We all do! But you know what? Her problems clear up after a nap. A *nap*! Can you imagine that? Give the girl a nap, and like *that* she's restored! Perfect. Beautiful. Luminous."

And as those familiar maracas from "Sympathy for the Devil" finally come shaking through the Monsoon speakers, find yourself suddenly aware of everything that's possible. And know that you can wait as long as it takes for her to understand that you're not going anywhere. Children or not, you'll wait for her to move beyond her affliction. You'll wait for her as an insect waits.

The view out the window will seem perfectly natural as you drive along 295 toward Long Island. Toward Sonja's house, where you'll have six months to wait it out with her before her parents return. There wasn't even a choice. The Jetta took its own course. Veered left without an argument.

So you passed up a ripe opportunity out in LA. So what? If you can wait for Sonja, then your career can wait for you. Surely there'll be other breaks. In the meantime, look on the bright side (as you've seen, there's always a bright side): Now you've got the perfect ending for your script.

Smile at the thought of this. Roll down the window. Catch some snowflakes on your tongue. Let the steering wheel go and play air drums for a few seconds on the dashboard. Sing along with Mick:

Ooo, who, who
Ooo, who, who
Ooo, who, who
Ooh, who, who
Oh yeah—what's my name!

Wonder how the sump pump is doing down in Sonja's basement. In a couple of hours you'll be able to check it out for yourself. You'll be able to smell the mildew firsthand. To once again touch the new banister that almost cost Merrill his marriage.

Roll up the window. Speed past the bright metallic-blue sign on the side of the road: WELCOME TO LONG ISLAND.

There's no turning back now.

And why would you want to? Now that you finally have your ducks in a row.

ACKNOWLEDGMENTS

Thanks to all those who helped get me through the first couple of novels, screenplays, TV pilots, and cryptic puzzles that will (thankfully!) never see the light of day. Especially Carl Johnson and Tom Toce, whose invaluable eyes guided me through misspellings and clichés of hysterical magnitude. My parents, whose infectious love of laughter, of books, of storytelling, inspired me to put keyboard to screen. Also helpful and deserving gratitude are the eager readers of my training wheels: the Bernstein-Bunzl clan, Bizzy Frankenberger, Juliet Heller, Tom Snyder, Bernie Wideman, Mary Clark, Amy Rosenthal, Heather Haber, Mer Broussard, Kay Rothman, KerenG, Jami Attenberg, Stephanie Kaplan, Jenn Bank, DDvonPP, Kim Cherovsky, my beary bro, Marc Israel and my own therapist, Fran Bernfeld.

This book: Matt Belinkie, Dawn Menzel, Michele Asselin and Dahlia Roemer need thanking. The good people at Random House: Shona McCarthy, Sarina Evan, and Brian Mclendon. Extra-special thanks to author and friend Lybi Ma. She was there for every word, every paragraph—every day. My agent: Emilie Stewart, whose unabashed enthusiasm needs to be bottled and attached to this book in a red net. And then, of course, Danielle Durkin—who was accosted by a stranger on the 4-train to Brooklyn one day and took a bold leap of faith. I really don't know what I'd do without her.

DAVID ISRAEL lives in Brooklyn, where he will die one day. His music has been performed extensively throughout the United States and in a dozen countries worldwide. This is his first novel. A longer bio, including some of the more embarassing moments of his life, can be found on his official website: *www.davidisrael.net.*

ABOUT THE TYPE

This book was set in a digital version of Monotype Cution. The original typeface was created by Ella Cution (1845–1910). Before becoming a punch cutter with her own chain of type foundries in cities as diverse as Constantinople and Istanbul, she was apprenticed to a midwife where she is said to have spent the better part of her days waiting for the invention of the disposable diaper.

It was there, working in midwifery, that Cution invented her first typeface: C Section. The following month, with money borrowed from her father, she opened her first type foundry. Despite ongoing problems with various labor factions (Active and Transition labor lobbied for shorter hours, while Induced labor fought for higher wages) she opened a dozen more within five years.

Sadly, after Ella Cution's passing, her franchise of type foundries was taken over by her daughter, Elektra Cution, and quickly flipped for the more lucrative Blimpie's chain, popular with many lunch and dinner patrons on the go.

8862